SLICE OF DEATH . . .

The whore was lethally effective as she swung back her leg and kicked out so that the toe of her high-buttoned boot heel hit the kneeling man under the chin. There was an audible crack as the blow splintered his teeth and he sprawled on his back, semi-conscious.

"That's nice, my sweet," she cooed, coming in closer, measuring her target, then hiking up the ruins of her dress and kicking the Chinese a second time. As her foot landed with a dull sound precisely between his thighs, the Oriental made a valiant effort to scream, doubling up, his hand pressing at the center of his pain, retching as he fought for air.

"Now for the last lesson," she said, lifting her skirt again, showing Cuchillo her tattered stockings with bright red garters and the flash of white lace on her drawers as she dropped with both knees on the chest of the last attacker, pinning him helplessly to the planking.

She still held the curved razor in her right hand, and she reached down with her left hand, tugging at the short queue of black hair that sprang from the Chinese's head, pulling back so that the stretch of his throat was exposed to her. There was a blur of movement and the unforgettable sound of a very sharp blade parting human flesh. Blood splattered to the side and she dodged nimbly off the chest of the dying man, folding the razor after wiping it on his jacket. Her breathing was calm and measured, and Cuchillo admired her, realizing that he was, indeed, in the presence of a remarkable woman. . . .

THE APACHE SERIES:

- #1 THE FIRST DEATH
- #2 KNIFE IN THE NIGHT
- #3 DUEL TO THE DEATH
- #4 THE DEATH TRAIN
- #5 FORT TREACHERY
- #6 SONORA SLAUGHTER
- #7 BLOOD LINE
- #8 BLOOD ON THE TRACKS
- #9 THE NAKED AND THE SAVAGE
- #10 ALL BLOOD IS RED
- #11 THE CRUEL TRAIL
- #12 FOOL'S GOLD
- #13 THE BEST MAN
- #14 BORN TO DIE
- #15 BLOOD RISING
- #16 TEXAS KILLING
- #17 BLOOD BROTHER
- #18 SLOW DYING
- #19 FAST LIVING

ATTENTION: SCHOOLS AND CORPORATIONS
PINNACLE Books are available at quantity discounts with bulk purchases for educational, business or special promotional use. For further details, please write to: SPECIAL SALES MANAGER, Pinnacle Books, Inc., 271 Madison Ave., Suite 904, New York, NY 10016.

WRITE FOR OUR FREE CATALOG
If there is a Pinnacle Book you want—and you cannot find it locally—it is available from us simply by sending the title and price plus 75¢ to cover mailing and handling costs to:

Pinnacle Books, Inc.
Reader Service Department
271 Madison Ave.
New York, NY 10016

Please allow 6 weeks for delivery.

____Check here if you want to receive our catalog regularly.

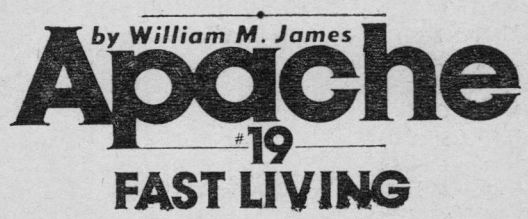

PINNACLE BOOKS   **LOS ANGELES**

This is a work of fiction. All the characters and events portrayed in this book are fictional, and any resemblance to real people or incidents is purely coincidental.

APACHE #19: FAST LIVING

Copyright © 1981 by William M. James

All rights reserved, including the right to reproduce this book or portions thereof in any form.

An original Pinnacle Books edition, published for the first time anywhere.

First printing, February 1981

ISBN: 0-523-40696-F

Cover illustration by John Alvin

Printed in the United States of America

PINNACLE BOOKS, INC.
2029 Century Park East
Los Angeles, California 90067

This is for Colin Murray, with overdue thanks for his tolerance of writers' neuroses. He's a good editor and, I hope, a friend.

"A bad editor kicks away the crutches of an author—a good editor is there to pick them up again."

Lobkowitz, *Publishers*
—*The Least Necessary Evil*

And by his smile, I knew that sullen hall;
By his dead smile I knew we stood in Hell.

> —Wilfred Owen, "Strange Meeting."

CHAPTER ONE

Before leaving the area the next morning, Cuchillo Oro crept from his hiding place near the ill-fated railroad and looked a last time at the remains of Pine's Peak. The people would come back to bury their dead, but that would be all. Nobody would ever bother to try to rebuild the township.* There wasn't any reason to.

But among the blackened ruins there was one person moving. A tall, grey-haired man, wearing a silver badge in his lapel. A badge that, even as the Apache watched him from the hillside, the sheriff took off and threw down in the trampled dirt of the main street, where the morning sun flickered brightly off it. Then he straightened up and looked around, thumbs hooked in his gun belt.

Cuchillo had the rifle and there was a passing temptation to gun the lawman down where he stood, but the Apache ignored it. He had a grudging re-

---

* This is the ending of the previous book in the Apache series, *Slow Dying*.

1

spect for the white man, seeing him as being less guilty for what had happened.

And there was some depth to Mann that he recognized. He was a tough, lonely, brave man, and Cuchillo had no wish to kill him.

"Hey, Apache! Golden Knife!" called out Thaddeus Mann suddenly, his voice ringing back from the hills around.

Cuchillo didn't reply, flattening himself in case it was a trap.

"I know you're there. I can think like you, Apache. I done some fighting in my days. I know why you done this. Can understand it, son. Really can. Town was dying and you just slammed down the coffin lid on it."

Cuchillo started to move slowly away, toward the west and the high mountains. But he could still hear the voice of the elderly lawman, shouting to the morning.

"You know what I got to do. I got to come after you. This was my town. Mine! You killed it, and lots of folks. I got no choice. I'll hunt you down, Cuchillo Oro. You hear me? You hear me?"

The big Indian paused on a gaunt crag, looking back. On an impulse he drew the golden knife and turned its gleaming blade so that the sun bounced off it, catching the eye of Thaddeus Mann.

"Yeah. I see you, I see you, Cuchillo. I'll play your game, boy. Play it right on through. You got a good lead, 'cos I got me things to do. Knots to tie tight and doors to close for good. Then I'll come after you."

The voice became fainter as the warrior padded on, ahead of the chasing sun, not bothering to look back again, but still hearing the last words of the lawman.

"It's not over, Cuchillo. Not over. This . . . isn't . . . the . . . end . . . not . . . the . . . end."

It wasn't.

CHAPTER TWO

Time has passed.
If you had been listening you could have heard it slipping by, carried on the melting water of the Sierra rivers, crumbling in the dust of the deserts. Days leaped across the sky from east to west, passing through the greyness of winter to the greening of spring, on into the warm sunshine of early summer.

Nearly six months gone since the lone Apache, Cuchillo Oro, legendary carrier of the great golden knife, had left the smouldering ruins of the Colorado township of Pine's Peak.

Left the settlement a raw head and bloody bones, with many of its inhabitants dead. It was the payment for a debt of horror and violence that Cuchillo had been unable to leave. Only one man had been sufficiently concerned about the dying of the township, and that had been the aging sheriff, Thaddeus Mann. He was sufficiently concerned to want to go after the Indian who had destroyed Pine's Peak, not because he specially liked the township, but because it was his job.

Thaddeus Mann had been an officer in the Civil War. Captain Mann of the Confederate States Army still had rending nightmares of the horrors he'd witnessed, nightmares that included his wife, the young and beautiful Rachel Ashley, who'd been burned to death in Richmond. All of that combined to make Thaddeus Mann a hard and unforgiving person, good at following the law, but not filled with the milk of human kindness.

And it was Mann who'd vowed vengeance on Cuchillo Oro. Mann who'd once been a bounty hunter south of the border, in Sonora. Mann who had turned grey early in life, somewhere between Richmond and the year he spent as a scout and Indian fighter west of the Mississippi, where he'd earned his nickname of Silver Wolf.

Golden Knife and Silver Wolf.

On the run from the ruined settlement, Cuchillo had headed west. Then he moved slowly southward, knowing from what he'd seen of Mann that he could prove to be a dangerous enemy, the kind of hunter who would follow a trail regardless of the cold or the difficulties or the danger. It had been bad enough during the long years of Cuchillo's feud with the white-eyes cavalry officer, Cyrus Pinner. That was a feud that had scorched across the Southwest and provided the land with its own legend of hatred.

Now Pinner was gone, and the big Apache knew that he was as close to freedom as an Indian could be. His name and description weren't on any of the law's flyers. He wasn't a wanted man. There were no crimes outstanding against him.

He suspected that Thaddeus Mann would do nothing within the law to track him down and bring him to trial. That would mean the full tale of what had happened in Pine's Peak being heard in court and Mann wouldn't take kindly to that. No. He'd seen the lawman throw down his badge of office, renouncing everything it stood for. When he came after Cuchillo it would be as man to man.

Cuchillo wondered how long it would be before the grey-haired wolf tracked him down.

It was quicker than he'd thought.

"I always done more'n my share of layin' women. Plenty more."

"You!" A cough of laughter that turned into a hawking burst of spittle, aimed at the overflowing brass jar, missing it by several inches, splattering the floor.

"Yeah. Me."

"Sure. If'n you had a twenty-dollar piece you couldn't get yourself a girl in a Juarez whorehouse!"

"By God, Jubal. You got a mouth bigger than a town outhouse." A pause as a further idea came creeping into his brain. "And it's 'bout as sweet."

There was more laughter from the dozen men in the small saloon. The arguing and joshing had been going on between the two card players for nearly an hour, each trying to top the other. But as the whisky flowed in, so the level of wit sank.

Sitting alone in a corner, Cuchillo Oro had been observing and listening for some time, sipping at a glass of warm beer, a greasy plate in front of him. There were a few crumbs left that showed the Apache had been eating a meal of tacos with some sourdough bread. There were still plenty of places around the Southwest where an Indian would have been refused service. If he was lucky that was all he'd get. But in Kimmel Creek they didn't much mind. As long as a man was sober—and that meant not mean drunk—then he was welcome. And if he had a few dollars to sport on a game of chance, then that was even better.

But Cuchillo was almost out of money. If he had a weakness it was for the cheap, fiery liquor served in bars in frontier towns. It was something that his only true friend among the whites, the little teacher, John Hedges, had warned him against. And most times the Apache steered clear of drink, hating the loss of control and the unsteadiness of hand and brain, the sickness that generally followed, with a gut-racking pain, and then the soreness the next day, blinking at the light. But every now and again it was good to shrug off self-control and relish the brightness that took over for a time. Yet Cuchillo also knew that such times presented him with the greatest danger.

With a heavy drinking session only two days behind him, the Indian was still feeling fragile, and his small pile of dollars had shrunk away almost to nothing, disappearing like the dew in the morning.

"Last time you tried to get laid you fell over gettin' out of your pants and got splinters in your cock."

"That's another damned lie! I won't have it. Tryin' to make me look like I'm some sort of damned fool."

"Don't take no makin', Eli, and that is the honest word."

"Jubal! I'm warnin' you!"

The skinny little man leaned back, nearly toppling from his chair, hooking his spurs behind the leg of the battered table, looking around the room to enjoy the laughter at his friend's expense.

"Warn away, Eli. Warn away."

The other man was below average height, but unusually fat. Rolls of sweating flesh hung pinkly beneath the layers of chins. His little eyes were almost buried from sight. He wheezed as he started to stand, then changed his mind and stayed where he was.

"I'll cut out your heart, Jubal Howell, you son of a bastard little runt."

"You just try that, Eli Edson, and see where the hell it gets you."

Cuchillo watched, emotionless, wondering whether the two men were drunk enough to actually try to get to blows. Both of them carried battered Army Colts jammed into worn holsters, typical working tools for cowboys and ranch hands, that might be used to shoot a coyote in the morning and hammer in fence posts in the afternoon. Nothing fancy about either gun. Eli and Jubal weren't the sort of men who would bother with hand-tooled Mexican rigs, cutaway and greased with feather-triggered pistols tied low on the thigh. If they started to shoot at each other it would take them two or three seconds to get their guns drawn and cocked and aimed.

The Apache smiled thinly at the spectacle, seeing the rest of the whites also nudging each other at the prospect of a battle.

"Even that damned Indian's laughin' at you, Jubal. Look there."

Every head swiveled to look at Cuchillo Oro, barely visible in the dark corner of the flyblown room.

"Him?"

"Yeah. Guess the Apaches have heard about you and your tiny cock, Eli!"

"Jubal, I'll . . ."

"Ain't me laughin' like a spooked mule, Eli. It's the Indian."

Suddenly the atmosphere in the saloon changed. The laughter stopped as if someone had turned off a faucet and there was shuffling of feet. Behind the chipped bar top the owner of the saloon checked his monotonous polishing of a long glass, putting it gently down as if it were a fine piece of Oriental porcelain.

Cuchillo felt the hostility—he'd had more experience of it than most over the last few years—and shifted slightly in his chair, bringing his own Navy

Colt more forward, ready for his left hand if he needed to drop down for it.

"You grinnin' at me, Indian?" barked Eli Edson, turning round with a sigh of anger, his shoulders nearly bursting from his tight blue shirt.

"I was not smiling," said Cuchillo, picking his words carefully, trying hard not to give offence, but knowing that if they wanted trouble, not all the talking in the world would hold it off.

"He talks pretty, don't he?" sneered the man behind the bar, eager to align himself with the rest of the room in case there was any comeback in his direction for serving the tall Apache in the first place.

Edson stood up, swaying a little, beer belly forcing out his belt. His cheeks were flushed and an unpleasant grin hung on the corners of his blubbery lips. He straightened himself, squaring his shoulders. Jubal Howell also stood, and the two middle-aged men stared at the Apache.

Cuchillo was becoming angry, not so much with the whites, but with himself. Angered that he had allowed his self-discipline to slip and let a smile through at the idiocies of the card players. Now he was involved in something that might well lead to violence, and could so very easily topple over the edge from farce into black tragedy.

"He sure is a big bastard, ain't he, Jubal?" said Edson.

"Maybe got a white pa. You a breed, boy? I'm talkin' to you, 'pache!"

"I hear you."

"Then how 'bout an answer?" called another man, a lean, squinting, clerkly man, in an Easterner's suit.

"I was sitting and eating and drinking. I had not wished to cause offence." He picked his words as carefully as if they were shreds of silk caught on the spines of a great saguaro cactus.

"You a breed?"

The question was repeated by Jubal Howell, tongue flicking out nervously across his dry lips at the prospect of some excitement. Some good safe excitement with a stinking Indian. Looked like he was carrying a gun, but that didn't signify. Left-handed. With a big knife, too. Difficult to see properly in the darkness where he was sitting very still. But that didn't signify either.

"Never met a poxin' Indian that could shoot worth a damn," sneered Edson.

"That's right," said the barkeep. "Put him in a barn and lock the door and he wouldn't hit the walls with a scatter-gun."

"Damned right, Pat. Damned right, you good old boy, you."

Howell looked again at the Indian. Broad shoulders and a handsome, flat face. Deep-set eyes that he couldn't rightly read, seeing them as chinks of reddish light at the bottom of black hollows. He wore standard Apache clothes. But his hair was tied up under a scarf, so it was impossible to see how long it was. He'd ridden in on a nondescript bay mare that was tied up outside the saloon.

"If you wish it, I will leave," said Cuchillo, his voice harsh with the strain of controlling the white rage that was rising in him.

"Maybe we do, and maybe we don't."

"I will go," the Apache decided, standing slowly, keeping his hands away from his weapons.

"Jesus Christ, but he is a big bastard, ain't he?" sighed Edson. "Maybe we ought to cut him down to size some."

"Old Jed's bullwhip'd do that real fine," said the little man, sniggering at the idea.

"Yeah. Indian comes in among white folks and don't behave, then we got us a right to educate him into some proper manners." Howell looked around, seeing that the support was there. "Maybe a good floggin' out front there. Call the children and women to see what we do."

"No," said Cuchillo, his voice so quiet that it barely disturbed the ripples of dusty sunlight that streamed through the open doors at the front of the building.

"How's that?"

"I said you would not whip me."

"Well . . ." whistled the saloon-owner. "That don't beat all."

The room was suddenly silent. Outside they could hear a child calling out to a friend, and the faint clopping of horse's hooves, coming slowly closer.

But none of them paid any attention to the distant sound. All of them were fascinated by the impending death of the Apache. For every moment that passed made his dying more certain.

"I have said that I will go. If you do not wish that and if you try to stop me then there will be killing. I warn you all." Cuchillo was controlling his anger, slipping into a fighting coolness.

"You're more damned uppity than a New Orleans nigra, Indian," said Eli Edson, shaking his head in mock appreciation. "I swear you are."

"Guess we better all go outside and set to teachin' this big buck a lesson in the kind of manners white men use."

Cuchillo looked at Howell, face impassive. "I have learned lessons from you whites, and none of them have been worth a pile of dried buffalo chips."

One of the watchers laughed, genuinely amused. "You take the prize, Indian. Leave it to me I'd say ride on off. Man with that much gall deserves a while longer to live."

"No," snapped Edson. "I say let's hang the bastard! He's too damned uppity to go on breathin' the same air as decent folks."

"Reckon you just committed suicide as sure as putting a bullet through the top of your head, Apache," said the other speaker.

"I will kill anyone who tries to take me," said Cuchillo, shifting his feet a fraction to make sure his balance was just right. His eyes raked the row of men, looking for any who seemed especially dangerous. But there were no obvious shootists among them. No cold-eyed bounty hunters liable to wipe him away before he could even draw.

They were just a crowd of friends and companions, enjoying a laugh and a drink, with the prospect of some extra entertainment at his expense. Cuchillo wondered how far any of them would be prepared to go. How high a price would they be prepared to pay for his life?

"You'll have to kill us all, then," mocked Edson.

By the look on their faces, the Apache wasn't certain that the fat little man and his friend had the room behind them.

"No. I will not be able to do that. There are too many for me. But I can kill you and you . . ." pointing at the two of them. "And perhaps two others."

"You figure?" laughed Howell.

"Yes."

The word was flat, as heavy as a stone falling to the bottom of a dry well, and it had the impact he knew it would. The movement of the rest of the whites wasn't very obvious, but there was a slight shuffling sideways to get out of the line of fire.

Howell and Edson failed to notice what was happening and they grinned nervously at each other, moving a little apart, the thinner one wiping the back of his hand across his sweating forehead.

"We goin' to have to take him, boys," said Edson, a crowing note of triumph in his voice.

The room stank with excitement, overlaying the

smell of all frontier saloons: sweat and piss and blood. And fear.

"I will not go," repeated Cuchillo Oro, ready for the move.

It came first from Edson, with Howell a half second behind. Both men reached down for their pistols, the drink making them even slower than they would normally have been. Cuchillo had never fancied himself as being a great hand with a gun, but he was way faster than the two middle-aged cowboys.

He drew his Navy Colt and fired four shots. The first bullet hit Edson just two fingers above his belt buckle. It plopped into the rolls of fat, leaving only a small dark hole in his faded shirt. Though it was only a thirty-six it was enough to send him staggering a pace back, starting to double up with shock. The air whooshed from his lungs. His hand, barely grasping the butt of his own Colt, dropped it and snatched at his wound.

The second bullet hit him in the throat, ripping his neck apart in a welter of streaming crimson, kicking him on his back in the spilled beer and sawdust, boots scraping at the floor. The beginnings of a scream came from Edson's mouth, before it was drowned in blood and he started to choke.

Jubal Howell was aware that his friend had been hit, hearing the boom of the Indian's gun, seeing Edson totter on his heels. But he was too busy trying to get his own pistol out and cocked. By the time Cuchillo fired a third time the cowboy was nearly ready for him, the handgun aimed, finger on the trigger. He'd done his best and it wasn't good enough.

It was a hell of an epitaph for a man to carry with him into eternity.

Both of the Apache's bullets aimed at Howell hit him in the chest, the first going clean between ribs and lodging in the vertebrae of the spine, cutting all the main links between brain and body. The fourth slug smashed into the ribs, splintering the bones, flattening the lead so that it sliced like a thrown razor through the walls of the heart. There was a great gush of blood from Howell's chest as he fell, rolling half on his side and lying still next to the dying Edson.

Nobody moved for a moment, stunned by the sudden eruption of death in their midst. None of them had really imagined that the skirmish would be so brief and bloody and total, nor that the Indian would beat both Edson and Howell.

And kill them both.

The hooves had stopped somewhere near and Cuchillo caught the sound of boots ringing out on the boardwalk, spurs jingling. But he was more concerned with what was happening inside the saloon.

He had two bullets left in the pistol, and there were nine or ten whites left facing him. Nobody moved, though the runty man whistled slowly between his teeth, a long, mournful note that went on and on.

"I kill the first man to move. I gave warning to them and they . . ."

The barkeep made his play, swinging up an old twin-barrel scatter-gun, cocking it and pointing it toward the Indian.

"You fuckin' bastard!" he yelled.

Cuchillo swung and snapped off a single shot, hitting him through the right shoulder. Good shooting from the hip in poor light at better than fifteen paces. The man yelped and dropped the gun with a clatter, holding his wound, blood dripping black between his fingers.

One of the other men spoke, clearing his throat first. "I counted five, Indian. You got one under the hammer or maybe you carry but five. Save flashin' them all off. Even if you got one left, there's . . . nine. Nine of us here. Odds don't favor you."

"Cuchillo says that even among jackals there is a leader. It is you who I kill first."

"Maybe. Maybe not, boy. You gone too far here. Those two men had friends. Guess we have to kill you."

"I did not wish for a fight. I said not. I said I would go. I could not do more."

"Killer!" spat another man. They were breaking from a group into a spread half-circle, giving him no clear target.

The sound of feet outside had stopped, as if the man had paused beyond the door of the saloon. Cuchillo considered turning and making a run for it, but there could be a dozen bullets in his back before he reached the safety of his horse. And there was the stranger outside. . . .

"Guess we'll give it to him, boys. No point in delaying," said one of the men.

Cuchillo had decided to shoot one in the center of the group and dive for the side window, hoping to reach the cover of the brush around Kimmel Creek. But he knew what a forlorn hope it was.

Before he could move there was the boom of a shotgun from behind him and he knew the stranger had come in to play his hand in the final reckoning.

Even the forlorn hope had gone.

CHAPTER THREE

"First man brushes leather gets his face separated from his skull with the other barrel," said a voice.

Cuchillo didn't look around. Didn't need to. He knew the voice well enough.

"Good day to you, Sheriff Mann," he said, eyes fixed on the watching whites.

"Not sheriff no more, Cuchillo Oro," replied the voice. "You know that. Saw me throw the badge. You took my town away."

"It was because—"

"I know 'bout that. I ain't proud about what happened back yonder. Town was dying, slow. You just pushed it some."

"Hey!" called the barkeep, still busy tying a dirty cloth around his wounded shoulder, helped by another man. "Just who the hell are you, mister? Comin' in here and buttin' in where you ain't wanted?"

"And what did you say this bastard's name was?" asked the skinny man.

Cuchillo still hadn't turned, knowing that he

would be blasted down by Mann if he tried anything clever. If he tried anything at all.

"Name's Thaddeus Mann. Late captain in the Confederate States Army. Late peace officer in the settlement of Pine's Peak, up in Colorado."

"So what's your part in this?"

"This Apache, he's a Mimbrenos and his name's Cuchillo Oro. Means Golden Knife, after the big blade he carries. Used to be a loner, called Pinner's Indian by some. On account of a long feud with a Yankee cavalry officer of that name."

"Pinner's Indian!" The word ran around the whites like the summer wind through prairie wheat, from man to man.

"And he came to my town. *My* town. There was some trouble and killing. And—"

"I was taught by a fine teacher, John Hedges, Mann. And what you have said is called an 'understatement,' is it not? Some 'trouble.' There was torture and rape. Babies murdered. But they were only Utes, so it did not matter."

"Mattered to me, Cuchillo," replied Thaddeus Mann, stung by the Indian's words.

"You did nothing."

There was no reply to the flat accusation. The saloon owner came out from behind the bar, arm now in a makeshift sling. "I figure you ought to—"

Mann's voice didn't change. "One more step and you'll lose the other arm, mister. Stand real still. And I feel that there's some folks there gettin' a mite itchy. Be a mistake to start scratching. This Indian burned down the town. Killed—killed a whole lot of folks. Better than a dozen. There was nothing left but a great scorched scar among the hills."

"But you said you didn't carry a badge. So what right do you—"

Man interrupted the speaker, the runty man. "I don't need no badge. I got all the authority I need right here in this scatter-gun, these pistols and the Winchester out on my horse. I owe a debt and I'll see it paid."

"Because of what he done?"

"Yes. Like an old friend of mine once said, there's some things a man can't ride around."

"So what do you intend? There he is. Why not just shoot him down?"

"Like you mob were goin' to do! It was a mob like you started all this trouble."

"He's ours now."

"No."

"You figure to take us all?"

"Cuchillo's got a single bullet left. I got the other barrel of this shotgun. That'll do a mess of damage to half of you. And there's twelve bullets in my pistols."

"You're an old man, Sheriff," said the little man, quietly.

"Might be some snow on the roof, but you could find there's one hell of a blaze in my belly. I could kill or wound the most of you. You believe that and there'll be no trouble."

A tall man with silver eyeglasses stammered out a

question from the back of the group. "Ppppardon me for asking this, Sheriff . . . bbbbut what do you aim ttto do with him?"

"I aim to kill him, mister."

"Then shoot, Mann," said Cuchillo. "There will not be a better chance."

"Not my way, and you know it. Not here. I caught up with you and I'll do it again. Now you go out there and get on your horse and ride on out."

"Hey, now . . ." began one of the watching men.

"What is it?" asked Mann, with a deceptive calm. "You got something to ask me?"

"Well, it don't seem right."

"It don't?"

"No. He killed two good old boys here and you're goin' to let him ride on free."

"He's mine, son. I'll go after him and I'll find him. Aren't that many places a six-foot Apache can hide in this fair land. I'll find him and I'll kill him. You can sleep easy on it."

"Talk does not cost dollars, Thaddeus Mann," said Cuchillo, still not turning to look at his enemy.

"But action does, huh? I'll be seeing you again, Indian. Now get the hell out of that door. Slow and easy, mind, and keep to the side. Less'n any of these gentlemen take it in their minds to do anything foolish."

"What will you do?"

"I'll wait an hour. No more."

"Then what?" shouted the barkeep, his face distorted by malicious anger. "You shoot us all down, that it?"

"No. Not unless I have to, mister. You all take off your clothes. Start now. Every last stitch. Beginnin' with the guns and belts. Then you can all lay down easy and still. Hour later I go out the door with your guns. Drop them in that trough I seen on the way in. And I ride on out."

"I'll get a posse after the both of you. Fuckin' Indian-lover!"

Mann shook his head. "Temper's a dreadful thing. And you want to get a posse after us—good luck to you. I know enough about Cuchillo Oro to be certain you'd not get within twenty miles of him. I done my share of trackin' in bare places. Lay ten dollars against a bent nickel you won't get close to me neither. Do yourselves a kindness."

"How's that?"

"Keep your time for buryin' these two. Cuchillo Oro."

"Yes?"

"You better go now."

"I thank you. I will do what I can to spare you if we should meet again."

He finally turned, seeing that Thaddeus Mann looked much as before. Tall, slightly stoop-shouldered. Grey-haired, with a low-crowned black hat. A face that was hard as granite. A face that didn't look as if it had experienced a lot of loving in the last few years. He was holding a scatter-gun, cradling it easily in both arms, and there were twin pistols in his belt, both Colt Army models, with butts polished to a dull gleam by use.

"You do not wish me to stay and help?"

There was the faintest ghost of a smile that flickered for a passing moment on the thin lips. "Day I can't handle a few drunks and cowboys is the day I lay down and pull the earth in on top of me, Apache. Get going. Next time I see you I'll kill you."

Cuchillo looked at the men. For a moment there was silence in the saloon. The blood was beginning to dry up around the edges, with a few flies gathering, dipping their feet delicately into the darkening crimson. The remaining whites were all slowly taking off their gun belts, dropping them reluctantly on the floor. One or two already had begun to undress.

"I will see you again, Thaddeus Mann," said the tall Apache.

"That's about the truth of it," replied the ex-lawman, his attention never wandering from his prisoners. "Just one hour."

"I go west."

"Figured you would."

"I had not said."

"Didn't need to. Hell, I guess I plain knew it all along."

The door of the saloon swung open and Cuchillo was out in the heat of the day, blinking at the sudden brightness, still holding his pistol. Across the street he saw a woman peering through a window. A little girl was hanging on her skirts, a long-barreled musket was in her hands. He waved at her and she ducked to one side, disappearing from sight.

As he heeled his horse out of Kimmel Creek, Cuchillo wondered whether he should have shot Thaddeus Mann in the back before leaving. But the older man had saved his life. The main reason, though, for not shooting him was that the Apache had only one bullet left and didn't want to take the chance.

So he rode on westward.

CHAPTER FOUR

Over the next month or so Cuchillo Oro ran into some good luck.
And into a deal of money.

Long years back Lieutenant Gabriel Moraga of the Royal Spanish Army was stationed at the Presidio in San Francisco. While out riding one day, doing some private exploring, he came across a tumbling river, the water breaking over heaps of round, white stones. Only they weren't stones. They were skulls. He named the place El Rio de Las Calaveras, the River of Skulls.

The name stuck and one of the original twenty-seven counties of California, founded in mid-February, 1850, was called Calaveras County. There were already crowds of miners rushing into the area, following the discovery of gold there two years before. And in 1854 the second largest nugget in the history of the world was found in the county, at Carson Hill, weighing in at one hundred and sixty pounds.

All around that part of the state small mining camps sprang up, some lasting only a few weeks, other staggering along for years. They were places of great hardship, with the possibility of rich pickings for anyone lucky enough to make the big strike. They were places where a woman might cost as much as a week's work for five minutes of her time, screwing behind a flapping curtain with the next man in line muttering for you to hurry up, and the next three dozen behind him thinking the same.

They were mining camps where they sold butter by the pint in summer and milk by the pound in winter. Where a man might get his throat slit for stealing a single egg and where the law was what men thought it ought to be.

And where men hardly gave a second glance to a tall Apache warrior, providing he didn't try to jump anyone else's claim, or cheat at cards.

Cuchillo Oro came to One Hundred Year Gulch a month after the killings at Kimmel Creek, and he stayed several weeks.

One Hundred Year Gulch was the third settlement of that name to have been built in the region within the last seven years. Each of them centered around a big silver strike, and each of them hoped to last at least a hundred years. The first strike proved to have been salted by an unscrupulous land agent and lasted eleven days. The second was on the very tail end of a seam and lasted something over thirteen months. The third of the Hundred Year

Gulches had already been in existence for over two years and currently showed no sign of running dry.

A measure of its success was that it already had both a school and a church, the former with a dozen inhabitants on weekdays and the latter with rather less on Sundays. There were also eight whorehouses, some of them doubling as saloons and rooming houses.

The township was a scattered collection of buildings, looking as though they'd been tumbled down from higher up the mountain in a great slide and had settled where they landed. There was little evidence of any kind of planning and the main street cut backwards and forwards like a drunk lurching from wall to wall in a narrow alley.

Unless you were very rich you lived near your diggings, among a raggle-taggle jumble of patched tents and makeshift huts. At night the air was crossed with the veins of smoke from battered metal chimneys and by day the hills were alive with the sound of metal on metal and metal on stone.

Cuchillo arrived at evening and he paused at the head of the pass, staring down the trail, catching the scents of cooking. The tall Apache was hungry but with only three dollars in his pocket, the end results of a couple of days horse breaking, he didn't have a lot of hope of getting both bed and board.

The sun was setting over beyond the tall mountains, throwing long shadows from the trees, cutting the sides of the hills into a checkerboard of light and dark. He walked slowly down the sloping length of the main street, dodging to one side as the body of a man came hurtling out of an open doorway, apparently thrown there by a huge woman who stood, arms akimbo, bellowing out a stream of colorful curses that would have done credit to a waterfront boss. She was wearing a corset of red satin, torn at the shoulder, hanging down and revealing one of a pair of massive breasts. Cuchillo paused and stared at her with frank admiration, ignoring the man in the dirt, who never moved.

"What you lookin' at, Indian?"

Cuchillo didn't reply, knowing from many bitter past experiences that contact with white women could often lead to all manner of trouble for himself.

"Never seen a tit before? I got me one t'other side even better an' bigger. Exceptin' for where Dutch Harknett took a piece out with his teeth five Christmases back."

Cuchillo smiled politely and started to move on, the voice of the woman following him, a raucous shriek like a demented parrot.

"You a fuckin' brownholer, Indian? Want to get you a look at my ass? More to your taste?" Seeing that he was not returning she waved a fist at him and turned back inside, pausing to spit with great accuracy in the upturned face of the unconscious man.

It was a fair and typical introduction to life in One Hundred Year Gulch.

* * *

The big Apache's main desire was to get something to eat. It would have been nice if he could have afforded a slug or two of the local rotgut, but that was beyond his means. Cuchillo's solitary weakness was a love of the white man's liquor and it had often dragged him into trouble before.

The noisiest saloon in the township was open for business, as it was for twenty-four hours each and every day out of the three hundred and sixty-five. From inside the scarred doors he could hear the jingling sound of a piano hammering out a discordant melody, and voices raised in song. There was the scream of a woman, and then bellows of laughter. As he walked towards the building there was the harsh noise of breaking glass. All in all, it seemed much like any other saloon that he'd ever visited.

It was a fair barometer of public opinion in any town that if the whores would accept an Indian, then anyone would. Prostitutes are among the most choosy and discriminating of folk.

A few heads lifted as he strode quietly in, easing himself through the crowd of miners around the long bar, ordering a beer. He turned away with it gripped safely in his good left hand, taking great care not to jostle anyone else. He had carefully tied his long black hair back, aiming at making himself appear more acceptable, and the gold-hilted knife was safely sheathed at the back of his belt, under the pale blue cotton shirt.

"You a breed?"

The question had no venom to it and he turned,

seeing a man a good foot smaller than himself, with pale, watery eyes that blinked a great deal. He looked somewhere in his late forties to middle fifties, dressed in a faded red shirt and blue pants. There was a swallow's eye neckerchief knotted around his throat under a prominent Adam's apple that jerked as he cleared his throat. He wheezed as he spoke and looked as if he were in the grip of some kind of wasting sickness.

"No."

"Full Indian?"

Cuchillo Oro nodded, sipping at his beer and wondering whether there was some way he could steal or borrow some money from this white man.

"Apache?"

"Yes."

"Mescalero?"

"No," sneered Chuchillo. "I am of the Mimbrenos tribe. The father of my father was our mighty chief, Mangas Colorado."

The little man's face didn't look as though he were very impressed by the name. It was a fact that the Apache had noted before in such surroundings; that in parts of the country, especially in the Southwest, everyone from the dribbling old man sunning himself on the porch to the little boy playing by his feet knew all about the land and its heroes and villains. But not in mining camps. The occupants of the boom settlements were frequently city dwellers, men who had thrown up dead-end jobs in offices and stores to head into the mountains with a deal of hope and precious little experience, chasing after the mother lode that would put all their previous drudgery behind them forever and open up lives of opulence, ease and arrogance. These men would never have heard of Mangas Colorado, would barely know of Cochise and Geronimo and Cuchillo Oro.

"That means the red shirt, doesn't it? I learned me some Spanish from a primer when I got out here. Somethin' to do nights."

The Indian turned away, leaning back against the bar, feeling the knife hard against his spine, the rough-cut jewels that decorated the hilt digging into him. His eyes ranged around the crowded room, seeing to his relief that his appearance had only created a passing disturbance. The card games had started again and the women were circulating, mechanical smiles pasted on their faces, their fingers spider-crabbing across the front of the men's trousers, looking for a response. The piano still played on and the air was heavy with drinking and loud talk.

"Can I buy you a drink, mister?"

Cuchillo looked back at the little white man, instinctively feeling his loneliness. It was a unique experience for him to be offered liquor in a saloon by a white and he almost smiled, catching himself in time.

"I thank you."
"Didn't catch your name, mister?"
"I did not throw it."
"What? Oh, I get it. Good, that one. Didn't throw

it, huh! Like it. My name's Christopher Devine. Friends call me Chris."

"I am called Cuchillo Oro."

He waited for the response. There was sometimes a look of bewilderment as if the name rang a distant bell. Or the old phrase about "Pinner's Indian" came out, recalling the time of the long and bitter feud with Cyrus Pinner of the United States Cavalry. But Chris Devine's face showed nothing but a polite interest.

"Knife of gold. Nice name. How d'you come by it, if'n you don't mind my asking?"

He was still trying to attract the attention of the elderly barkeep, down the further end of the room.

"It is my name, that is all."

"Can I call you Cuchillo? Or would you prefer Mr. Oro?"

"What you wish. I have been called many things in my time, not all good. I am happy with Cuchillo."

"Damned fine," spluttered the little man, clapping him on the shoulder. "And you call me Chris." Raising his voice, "How 'bout some service down here, friend?"

The bartender scowled at him, looking long and hard at Cuchillo. "I only got me two hands, and I ain't your fuckin' friend, mister. What's your pleasure?"

"Two more whiskies. No, make that four." He threw down a few coins in the beer that slopped all over the top of the bar.

"Well, Cuchillo, what brings a warrior like you to One Hundred Year Gulch?"

The Apache had never been very good at social small talk and he found it difficult to keep up his end of the conversation. But Devine didn't seem bothered by his lack of response, content to buy more drinks for them both and chatter on about himself. Where he'd come from—Rhode Island. What his job had been—teller in a small bank. His family—a wife dead of a bloody flux on their sixth wedding anniversary and two little children, both killed in a fire at their rooming house.

"Pretty girls, both reading by the fire in print dresses. Some embers fell out and they were both burned. I was nearly broken by that, wondering why the Good Lord had singled me out for such unhappiness. But, truth is, Cuchillo, my good friend, that I lacked the courage to kill myself and end it. Damned coward, that's me."

He was becoming very drunk and under normal circumstances Cuchillo would have been disgusted by the white's self-pity, but Devine had told him other things.

"I came here to get rich. Near done it, too. Not a big strike . . ." his voice dropped to a stage whisper, "but enough to keep me in comfort. Trouble is, Cuchillo, I can't trust a soul to help me work it. Not a soul. Nobody likes me. Nobody. They don't like me at all. But they don't know about the silver. Sure don't."

The Apache sipped with unusual control at his

own whiskey, taking care not to allow the insidious warmth to cloud his brain. Devine was obviously seeking help and seemed to have the money to pay for it. It would have been foolish to have ignored the opening.

And Cuchillo was nobody's fool.

Despite all the hints, the little New Englander wouldn't come right out with it and ask Cuchillo Oro to take the job as his partner.

He just kept on, slurring his words more and more, about how there were shootists around, mean bastards who wouldn't bother to work honest, who'd rather sit around and wait until a man like Chris Devine got himself a decent strike. Then they'd call in and persuade him to make it over to them.

"Persuade?" asked Cuchillo Oro.

"Sure. Damned good at persuadin', some of them good ol' boys. Use a twelve-pound sledge to add a mite of weight to what they say. Just lay that a few times 'cross your knees and you'd as soon play kiss their asses as not sign the papers."

"You can fight."

Devine laughed, the drink taking him over so that the laughter went on and on, rolling from him like an endless stream of ribbon, becoming almost hysterical. Until the Apache stepped away from him, fearing for his sanity.

"Guess you can," stammered the white man, fighting to regain control of himself. "You can fight. But they'll likely kill you."

"I asked you and you said nothing. Now I must teach you that Cuchillo Oro is not to be so treated."

The grip grew tighter and tighter, dragging Schultz to his knees, staring up in sick agony. There was the brittle snap of a bone breaking and the miner screamed, his voice surprisingly quiet and feeble for such a big man. Only then did Cuchillo let him go, pushing him away so that he fell, nursing his broken wrist.

"Bastard! I fuckin' kill you for dat! Oh, I fuckin' kill you, Indian."

The crack of the arm and the cry of pain had finally drawn everyone's attention to the scuffle, and the saloon had fallen silent, the man at the piano faltering along for a few more notes before he stopped playing.

"That Indian broke his arm. And must have strangled that little fellow." Cuchillo couldn't see who had spoken, the voice coming from the crowd at one of the card tables.

"It was him nearly choked that man," pointing at where Christopher Devine was struggling to his knees, hands clasping his neck as he fought for breath, doubled over, shaking his head in his distress.

"True. Oh, Jesus Christ. That devil German. Nearly . . . Indian saved me . . . my life. Oh . . ."

Schultz was helped to his feet by a couple of men, cradling his broken arm across his chest, color splashed on his cheekbones, the rest of his face white as death, eyes burning with vicious hatred of the silent Indian.

"I swear I kill you, Indian."

"Cuchillo says that all talking costs nothing, but to do what you say will have a high price."

An hour later and the saloon was just as it had been before. The German had left, still swearing a dreadful vengeance, his anger also aimed at little Devine, who shrugged it off, pouring himself three fingers of courage from the bottle offered by the suddenly sympathetic barkeep.

"I must go," said Cuchillo, after another couple of drinks had warmed him.

"Where?"

"Out. I have no money so I must go on."

"I'll pay you. Pay you well. Be my bodyguard, Cuchillo. And live in my shack."

The big Apache nodded without any hesitation. It wasn't the best job he'd ever taken, but it was a whole lot better than nothing.

Cuchillo was enough of a realist to know that, generally speaking, something was always better than nothing.

CHAPTER FIVE

For the next few weeks Cuchillo Oro did everything that Chris Devine wanted from him. He did some work in the diggings but mainly he made sure that he was around in case he was needed. They saw no sign of Schultz, unless you could call the half-ton boulder that came bouncing ponderously down the side of the hill for no seeming reason and nearly killed Devine a sort of a sign.

The Apache knew little about mining skills, but it was clear that Devine had a reasonable strike. Not big enough to take him out of work into easy street for the rest of his life, but good enough to guarantee setting himself up in a small business in a few months. Devine talked a lot about his plans and hopes to the tall Indian as they worked together, saying that there was a widow he'd met back in Independence who'd made kind of promises.

One evening, after he'd washed himself in one of the many small streams that veined through the rocks around One Hundred Year Gulch, the Rhode

Islander suggested that they might go into town and relax a little.

"Got me near three-quarters of what I need, Cuchillo. If'n I get enough, and the strike still runs, then I swear I'll deed it to you. You're a good man, and better than most whites I ever met. That's the damned truth."

So the two of them went into the township, picking their way between staggering drunks and soliciting hookers, going into the resplendent Twin Towers bar. Resplendent in that it had some shreds of carpet still on the floors. Cuchillo had been puzzled at how the saloon had earned its name, seeing that it was simply a frame box, like every other building in the settlement. Chris Devine had laughed his high-pitched giggle.

"On account of how it once had two necessaries out back. That was one more than any other bar. Only one left now. T'other burned down six months back."

They took a shot glass each from a stack on the top of the bar and walked over, the white man holding a bottle of whiskey by the neck, finding a quiet table in the corner. There wasn't the usual noisy activity; just a group of men clustered round the big card table in the middle of the room. Every now and again Cuchillo heard a collective sigh of despair, or a whistle of appreciation, as one or other of the players made a killing.

Devine looked across at the group, and the Apache saw something come into his eyes, something that was about halfway between lust and greed, like a man staring at a woman's breasts decorated with emeralds.

"What is wrong, Chris?" he asked.

"Wrong? Oh, just taking a look at that game. I played back home. Fact is, lot of my troubles came . . . But that's in the past now, I guess."

They carried on drinking, both content with their own thoughts. So much of Cuchillo's life had been spent alone that he was always happy not to talk. And Devine's mind was clearly wandering back again to the green-topped table and the flutter of the cards, the whispering of the onlookers and the jingling of dollars.

"I wonder if . . ."

The Apache almost smiled. The white men were so transparent in their desires, incapable of masking their minds as Indians could.

"I wonder if I might just walk over and watch. Just watch."

He pushed back his chair, stepping over to join the ring of men around the game. Cuchillo picked up the bottle, now four-fifths empty, and followed him. A few of the miners nodded to him, moving aside to let him through. The word of the way he'd broken the arm of big Karl Schultz using only his left hand had run round the diggings and nobody wanted to risk tangling with the massive Apache.

There were six men sitting in on the poker game, four of them that Cuchillo recognized and two strangers. One of the strangers looked like a city dude, in a black cutaway coat and lace around the front of his white shirt. The Apache looked carefully at this man, having seen professional gamblers before. The hands were too soft and pale, the nails trimmed and brushed, as if he had never done an honest day's work in his life.

"Hey there, Devine," said one of the players, standing up and gathering in the few dollars on the table in front of him. "Fancy coming in? I had my fill for the night."

Cuchillo also noticed that the largest pile of money was in front of the man with the soft hands. The life of a gambler in mining camps was often short. Few of them ever bothered to cheat. They knew the odds and could count cards. They were simply good poker players and in the long run they'd always come out ahead of a group of often drunk miners. That tended to make other men suspicious, to say the least, and many gamblers had found themselves dancing on thin air from the town's hanging tree for too much winning.

"I'm not sure."

The gambler looked up at him from soft brown eyes and smiled. "Guess we'd be proud to have some new blood in the game, Mr.—?"

"Devine. Christopher Devine."

"By God, but he's 'bout the richest of us all. Beaverin' away on his strike with that Indian guard of his."

The brown eyes turned towards Cuchillo, opening wider as they took in the height and build of the Apache.

"Broke a man's wrist just with his fingers, he did."

"That so?" murmured the gambler. "Then we must take care not to annoy him, must we not?"

"Come on, Chris," called another of the players. "See if you can bring us some luck."

"Maybe Cuchillo can bring me luck," replied the little man, taking the proffered seat, beckoning to the Indian to stand behind him.

And so the game went on.

"Three sevens beats them kings and queens, do they not?"

"Guess so."

"I figured you was bluffing, mister."

"And you were sadly correct, Mr. Devine. You're a player of some skill. I compliment you on it."

"It's Cuchillo here makes the difference. Brings me the luck I never did have before."

After an hour and a half there were only three of them left in the game. The money was changing hands so fast that it was difficult to keep track of it, but by Cuchillo's reckoning Devine was around four and a half thousand dollars to the good. The gambler was digging into his wallet and the other miner was just hanging on in there, staying out of the big pots and picking up forty or fifty dollars on the occasional smaller ones. The crowd around the table had swelled as word ran through the township of the high money game. It was unusual to see more than two dollars go on a hand, and here was several hundred going on a pair of tens to beat a pair of eights.

Devine was playing like a man inspired. He seemed almost to know what cards he was going to draw before they were dealt, picking the hands to bluff on and those to fold with. There was one occasion when he went all the way on a pair of deuces, finally making the gambler fold three nines against him.

"That Indian certainly brings you luck, Mr. Devine. So much so that I fear I am not going to be able to carry on filling your pockets with my silver for very much longer."

"Cuchillo's my lucky idol," smirked the little miner. "If I ever die, then he gets it all. And I'm sayin' that in clear sight of you all. What's mine is Cuchillo's. Best damned friend I ever had."

The Apache didn't say anything. With the kind of money that Devine had won, combined with all that was in the bank, he would have enough to stake himself to some good times. Maybe out on the coast. He'd been in San Francisco once before and it had seemed a pleasant place. If Devine hadn't been such a friendly, innocent man, there had been times in Cuchillo's life when the thought of that money would have been a sorry temptation.

But he liked Devine. Over his twenty-five years or so of living Cuchillo had only met a handful of whites that he had not actively disliked. First among them had been the diminutive schoolteacher back at the old rancheria, John Hedges, the man who had drummed the rudiments of reading and writing into the thick skull of the young Apache. It had been too long since he'd seen John Hedges. There had also been the redheaded young cavalry officer, Charlie Lovick.

The gambler stood up, trying unsuccessfully to mask his anger at having lost so many of his dollars, bringing the Apache's mind back to the present.

"I'm out, Mr. Devine." offering his hand and making the best of an ill job. "Been a privilege to play with you. Perhaps another day?"

"Yeah. Perhaps," grinned Devine, scooping the mountain of money towards him, trying to stack it into piles.

"How much?" asked a voice from the back of the jostling throng.

"Close to nine thousand dollars, near as I can figure," called a pale-faced man from the front, standing at Cuchillo's elbow.

"Drinks on the house," shouted Devine, forcing his chair back, turning to smile at Cuchillo. The Apache thought that he'd never seen such happiness on a human face.

The Two Towers was doing a roaring trade, the drinking and singing going on late that night. The miners all shared in Devine's happiness. Cuchillo had already noticed that they were a surprisingly tight-knit community, bonded together by their hardships, driven on by the occasional strike. The success of one miner meant prolonged hope for the rest.

"Hell, Cuchillo. I finally done it. Hear me? I finally done it. Pretty up and walking good, huh?"

Devine was euphoric, almost incapably drunk, hanging on the arm of the big Indian, feet stumbling around as though they didn't even belong to him. The pair had left the saloon to three resounding "Huzzahs" from the company there and were now walking through the still outskirts of the township, picking their way by the pale light of a new moon.

"You know, friend Cuchillo, that I honest and truly like you more than anyone I ever met. Guess I even love you. Yes." He tried to stamp his foot to add emphasis to his words but nearly fell. "Yeah. Love you, Cuchillo. Wouldn't never say that to another man. Not in my life. Didn't dare to. But you don't mind, do you?"

"I do not mind."

"That's good. Good. Positively excellent. Positively excellent." Devine liked the phrase so much that he rolled it twice more on his palate, savouring it as though it were the finest of French wines.

"You will put the money in the bank?"

"Sure."

"In the morning?"

"Guess so. Just don't take on so, old friend. Cuchillo Golden Knife Oro. Mr. Mimbrenos Apache. Goin' to be just fine. Couldn't be better, old friend. Positively excellently excellent."

They were nearing the tumbledown hut where they lived, the noise of the numerous streams drowning out the sounds from the settlement behind them.

Devine paused a moment, swaying like an aspen in a strong wind, still hanging on Cuchillo's arm, looking fuzzily up into his face.

"When we get back, I'm goin' to do somethin' for you. Never done it for nobody. No man. Guess you won't mind, old friend. Just want to do it and please you. Don't see no harm in that."

The Apache had no idea what Devine was babbling about, taking it for the idle chatter of a drunk. He smiled down at the little man and tried to move him on, putting one hand on his shoulder to steady his wobbling steps.

"Come, friend," he said.

"Never been so happy. Make you happy too. Know I'll be good at it. Happiest day I . . ."

Cuchillo felt the little man stumble and nearly fall, but he managed to stoop and support him.

"Careful."

"Sure, Cuchillo. Been damned funny if I'd fallen on my face just when I was saying about this bein' the happiest—"

The bullet missed the Apache by a couple of inches, passing by his cheek close enough for him to feel the hot sting. He felt the jerk and shudder as it hit Devane, somewhere in the upper part of the body, he guessed. Only then did he hear the crack of the rifle from among the trees up to the right of the tents.

"Oh, God, I'm killed, dear friend. Killed," muttered the little miner, lending action to his words by slumping in the arms of the Apache like a sack of grain, utterly devoid of life.

Cuchillo lowered him swiftly to the earth, seeing in the moonlight that it had either been an exceptionally good shot or an exceptionally lucky one in poor light, angled down.

The bullet from the hidden marksman had hit Devine in the upper left part of the chest, clean through the heart, killing him more or less instantly. Cuchillo never stopped to think whether it had been a quick death. All that concerned him was that murder had been done to a man he had grown to like and who had been employing him to help guard his life.

Suddenly there was a movement in the shadows, further to the left than where Cuchillo thought the shot had come from, and a man stepped out into the silver gleam.

He was holding a rifle steady on the kneeling Apache. "Don't make a move, Cuchillo," said ex-lawman Thaddeus Mann.

sagebrush. It was deep in black shadow, but he was certain there was movement and certain that . . .

His hand reached around, drawing the gold-hilted knife, feeling the familiar roughness of the uncut gems against his fingers. Drawing it in a hiss of lethal speed, he brought his left arm up and back, tensing himself for the throw.

"There," he whispered, turning every head in his direction.

The creeping figure was about sixty paces away—a monstrous distance to throw a knife. But the antique *cinqueda* was perfectly balanced, and Cuchillo had practiced long, long hours to make himself a master of it at any range. He knew how many times it would revolve, depending on the whip from his wrist that sent it whirring from him. The moon flickered for a moment off the polished metal.

"It looks like . . ." began someone, the words dying in his throat at the high drama.

They could all see the man—a burly figure in a plaid shirt, stumbling and carrying one arm awkwardly across his chest. In the sudden silence they could actually hear the smack as the point of the *cinqueda* thumped into the man's back, just below the neck. One hand went to the glittering hilt, as if he were trying to tug it loose, and his feet staggered.

"By God! It is . . ." began someone else.

"Schultz," said Cuchillo quietly, beginning to walk quickly toward the lurching man. He saw the rifle drop where the German had been trying to clutch it in his broken arm.

The Indian heard Mann asking the crowd who Schultz was, but nobody answered. They were too busy pushing each other and jostling after Cuchillo Oro.

Schultz tottered, head thrown back, still straining for the knife, spinning around like a painted puppet on the lid of a Swiss music box. And then he fell, slipping forward like a man entering deep water, lying on his face, boots scrabbling for a few moments at the earth before he was finally quite still.

Mann joined Cuchillo just after the tall Apache had tugged the golden knife free from the dead man's spine. "Thanks," he said.

"I pay all debts, Sheriff," replied the Indian.

"Yeah. So do I, Cuchillo. So do I."

CHAPTER SEVEN

In 1869, at Promontory, Utah, the Central Pacific and Union Pacific railroads were finally linked and the way was open clean across the land.

After leaving One Hundred Year Gulch, Cuchillo Oro traveled first eastward and then dodged north and back south, finally using some of the fourteen thousand dollars bequeathed to him by Christopher Devine to purchase a ticket on the train west, finishing up in the bustling, unruly port of San Francisco.

Cuchillo had left the mining camp the morning after the two killings, having collected all the monies owing to him. The manager of the small bank wasn't too happy about releasing Devine's roll on the say-so of a massive savage, but there was sufficient strength of feeling in One Hundred Year Gulch to cause him to change his mind with undignified rapidity.

And Thaddeus Mann?

The grey-haired hunter had managed a quiet word with Cuchillo that same morning, joining him at a table to share a meal of eggs and grits.

"That's one life each, son," he'd said.

"Yes."

"Can't go on like this."

"No."

"Savin' each other." He allowed himself a shadow of a smile. "Not the way it's supposed to be."

"I think not," said Cuchillo, using a hunk of a corn dodger to mop up some of the golden pool of egg yolk on his plate.

"Killin' is what I'm hopin' to do to you, son. And nothing changes that."

"I did not think it would, Thaddeus Mann. You are not that kind of person."

"Guess I'm not. More coffee?"

"Surely welcome. That knife of your'n surely saved my skin. Guess I'd have been strange fruit on their hangin' tree else."

"I had sworn to myself that I must slay the man who shot my friend."

"That little fellow? Yeah. I know what you mean."

"Cuchillo says that to give word is to keep word. There is no other way."

"I'll drink to that, son," replied Mann, lifting his mug of coffee, hot and black enough to float a horseshoe.

"What of today?"

"Today?"

"Will we fight here?"

Thaddeus shook his head, wiping his mouth on

the blue sleeve of his faded shirt. "Wouldn't hardly be proper. Nope. Wouldn't."

So they'd reached an agreement.

Cuchillo would be given two days grace. Until dawn on the day after next. But both of them knew that wherever the Apache ran, the sheriff would be slowly and inexorably on his trail.

It crossed Cuchillo's mind that he would do well to double back into the settlement and kill Mann from hiding before the chase even began. But an obscure respect for the older man stayed his hand.

Before the Indian rode off, Thaddeus Mann came out in the street to see him leave, calling out a warning to him.

"No more chances, Cuchillo Oro."

The Apache hadn't even bothered to raise a hand to acknowledge the words.

There wasn't any need.

In a booming town where a rented house could cost you a thousand dollars, a month, Cuchillo found his heavy roll wasn't going to take him very far. He spent the first day there arranging stabling for his horse and walking about the high, swooping hills, trying to get the feel of the place once more. He still kept his hair tied up, purchasing a narrow-brimmed, high-crowned hat to hide it. His cotton shirt and trousers didn't attract a second glance.

San Francisco had only just scraped itself back from the brink of total lawlessness, and it had taken two major vigilante movements to do it, with public hangings to deter the wicked. On his previous visit the Apache had learned of the self-styled Hounds, who had brought terror to the Chinese and Mexicans of the city, beating any male whose skin was not of the right color, and raping any woman. They were all the ragged scrapings from a New York regiment of soldiers who had moved west and they adopted bright uniforms with gold and lace and frills when they went on their vicious raids.

The other gang that had ravaged the waterfront areas of San Francisco were the Sydney Ducks, murderers and thieves from Australia. But in 1851 a Vigilance Committee was formed and managed in a short time to impose some kind of order.

However, between 1849 and 1856 the swelling city found itself with an average of a murder every two days. Again the doubtful face of citizens' armed patrols and semi-official hangings appeared, only to be finally dissipated in August of 1856 when the young governor of the state, J. Neely Johnson, made it clear that if they continued he would send in the troops.

Now, in the sixties, things had greatly improved. But it was still the sort of place where you could win or lose a fortune in a gambling house, eat one of the best meals the nation could provide, and secure the company for the night of a beautiful *fille de joie*.

Or get your throat slit for a silver dollar.

* * *

His first purchase, even before the hat, was a pistol. The reputation of San Francisco was such that in certain parts a man without a gun was in more danger than a man without breeches trying to vault a triple-strand barbed-wire fence.

It was a standard 1861, thirty-six caliber Navy Colt, a gun that he had always preferred to the heavier, forty-four Army model, liking the sweetness and tightness of the action. And the smaller bullet didn't make a whole lot of difference. If you hit a man straight enough he'd go down, whatever the caliber of the pistol.

He tucked it into his belt in his favorite place, at the back, letting his shirt hang outside the butt to cover it, but not in such a way that he couldn't get it out reasonably fast when he needed it.

Cuchillo never guessed that he would be using the handgun before he had been in the city for twenty-four hours. Not that he wasn't ready to use it all the time.

That awareness and constant hair-trigger mind was one of the reasons that the Apache had lived as long as he had.

It was around eight in the evening and he had made his way down off the sunlit peaks of the city towards the noisy waterfront. His money was in a leather belt buckled tightly under the shirt and he found it hard not to feel it constantly, to reassure himself that he, Cuchillo Oro of the Mimbrenos tribe, really owned, legally, the sum of thirteen thousand, eight hundred and forty-six dollars. Plus a few jingling cents. For that he could have bought himself most of the tribal lands of his people that the whites had been stealing over the years.

He was jostled several times and each time restrained himself from responding with violent action. It had been a long time since the Indian had been in a large city and he already found the air foul and the numbers of people around him crushingly oppressive.

As the wind began to rise from the west, he saw and smelled that most typical of all San Francisco experiences. First it appeared as a few pale, ghostly tendrils, feeling their way in over the dull waters of the Bay, rising and embracing the hills to the Pacific side of the city. Then it thickened and rushed in toward him with an eerie speed and silence, tasting wet and salt to his tongue, dampening his black hair.

Within ten minutes it seemed that the Apache was a man alone.

The fog wrapped itself around him like a suit of clothes about a long-drowned seaman, seeming to fill his ears with muffling stillness. Even with his keen eyesight he was virtually helpless, his tracking skills and wood-lore useless. The fog grew more dense by the minute until he could no longer even see the roofs of the houses that he walked by.

Ahead of him there was the dim sound of water lapping ceaselessly against the rotting wood of the piers and wharfs and Cuchillo checked himself, fearful of plummeting over the edge into the chill waters. Unusually for an Apache, he was a strong swimmer, but he had heard much talk on his earlier visit about the dangers of the ripping, swirling currents and became cautious.

Then he heard the cry of a woman in distress.

Normally Cuchillo would have paid little attention. If it had been a woman of his people, then he might have gone to her aid. But in such a place it would be a white woman. And experience had taught him that they were almost always shallow, vain, vicious animals who could be trusted no more than a trapped coyote.

But this was different. On the waterfront, in this thick fog, it was difficult to judge distances and directions. It would be easy to blunder into a fight without being aware of it. And Cuchillo had long learned that the best way of dealing with such situations was to confront them directly. So he drew the pistol from his belt and cocked it, walking forward cautiously, the gun probing the greyness, gripped tightly in his left hand.

"Help me! Oh, help me! You dogs!"

The wind came and went, making the visibility change from moment to moment, and it cleared the area of wharf for a few seconds, like the curtain at a theatre, showing a scene from a real-life drama. There were three Chinese men, Cuchillo saw, dancing cat-footed around a single figure, a tall woman, dressed in a long red dress, whirling to try to keep her back from the attackers. The Orientals all held knives with unusually long, narrow blades, flicking them out and back. The woman's dress was cut in several places and there was a feather of blood on her left arm. What surprised Cuchillo was that she also had a weapon, an open razor that she held professionally, the blade back across her knuckles, trying to get close enough to the Chinese to use it.

The Apache knew enough of the ways of the whites in such a city to be certain that no decent woman would be down on the docks at night alone, in a red dress, carrying a cutthroat razor for her protection.

"Whore," he said to himself, easing down the hammer on the pistol. Why should he bother with such a woman? Probably a diseased creature, tainted with illness and cast out from her decent fellows.

Yet there was something about the way she fought that touched his admiration. She was like a wounded deer, surrounded by snarling jackals, holding them off, knowing that in time their circling would wear her down and they would be in with pecking steel and the blood would flow and she would die.

The fog dropped down as the wind fell again, shutting him off from the fight, though he could still hear the padding of the Orientals' slippered feet on the wet wood and the harsh breathing of the woman. She had stopped calling out for aid, concentrating all her efforts on holding off the attackers.

He eased forward to where he knew they were, realizing that the shifting of the mist must have kept him hidden from them in the shadows. Surprise was worth an extra man in such a situation. He slipped back the hammer of the pistol, hearing the faint click, reaching across and pulling out the knife in his right hand.

There were great crates everywhere, some with wisps of sodden straw leaking from them. The Apache was able to creep from one to another, getting closer, taking his time, yet knowing that too much delay would be fatal for the woman.

At last he was close enough to see, even through the lowering curtain of fog, the flickering shapes of the Chinese, circling, faces turned from him. The woman's dress was hanging in strips from her waist, so that as she turned it flared out like a ribboned skirt, showing white thighs beneath. And there was more blood dripping from the end of her fingers. She was moving more slowly and Cuchillo could hear one of the Chinese giggling with excitement and anticipation.

The woman feinted towards the hiding Indian, and the nearest of her attackers stepped back. It was the one that giggled, hopping into the fog and disappearing for a moment from the woman's eyes. Even in her terror and exhaustion she was suddenly aware that he hadn't come back from the bank of darkness. But there was someone who . . .

"What . . . ?" she breathed. It was a stranger. A big, broad man, in a strange high hat.

The body of the giggling Chinese was laid carelessly behind one of the boxes, his throat slit with such savage power that the blade of the *cinqueda* had chipped the bones of his neck. He had never known what demon of blackness had taken him, lifting him effortlessly. There had been coldness below his chin and then warmth across his chest and stomach and then nothing.

Cuchillo's appearance was noticed by the other two Orientals simultaneously and they both checked their dervish whirling, facing him, gazing blankly at him. He leveled the Colt and pulled the trigger twice.

He was not a great shot with a pistol, but his first bullet was straight and true, hitting the man on the left in the center of his face, dissolving it to a mask of blood and shards of torn bone, pulping his nose inwards, the thirty-six ripping through his brain and kicking him backwards, arms flying out. He flopped down on the very edge of the wharf, so that his head and shoulders hung in space, the blood draining quickly into the Bay. The knife was flung from his hand, arcing high and vanishing into the dome of fog, finally splashing into the grey water.

As he fell the Chinese knocked into his surviving comrade, pushing him off balance, so that Cuchillo's second bullet hit him in the right side of his chest, high, near the shoulder, tearing through the thin black jacket he wore, burying itself in the bones of his upper arm. He dropped to his knees, whining with pain and shock, trying to hold the wound with his left hand, the knife a silver streak on the wood at his side.

The Apache cocked the gun again, leveling it at the Oriental's head, but a call from the woman checked him from firing.

"No. Leave him to me."

"I can shoot and—"

"No, mister. I'll thank you proper in a moment, but now I aim to settle for that dirty little yellow bastard in the only way him and his soddin' brothers understand."

She was lethally effective, stepping in and swinging back her leg, kicking out so that the toe of her high-buttoned boot hit the kneeling man under the chin. There was an audible crack as the blow splintered his teeth and he sprawled on his back, semiconscious. His legs were apart, arms spread, blood glistening on his clothes.

"That's nice, my sweet," cooed the whore, coming in closer, measuring her target. She hiked up the ruins of her dress and kicked the Chinese a second time. This time her foot landed with a dull sound precisely between his spread thighs. Even Cuchillo winced at the force of the impact and the Oriental made a valiant effort to scream, doubling up, his hand pressing at the center of the pain, retching as he fought for air.

"Teach the slit-eyed sod. Now for the last lesson."

Lifting her skirt again, showing Cuchillo her tattered stockings with bright red garters, and the flash of white lace on her drawers, she dropped with both knees on the chest of the last attacker, pinning him helplessly to the planking.

She still held the curved razor in her right hand and she reached down with her left hand, tugging at the short queue of black hair that sprang from the Chinese's head, pulling back so that the stretch of his throat was exposed to her. There was a blur of movement and the unforgettable sound of a very sharp blade parting human flesh. Blood splattered to the side and she dodged nimbly off the chest of the dying man, folding the razor after wiping it on his jacket.

"Should cut his cock off and shove it in his evil mouth," she said in a calm conversational voice, as though she was discussing whether a seedcake could have done with a touch more sugar. Her breathing was calm and measured and Cuchillo admired her, realizing that he was in the presence of a remarkable woman.

The fog cleared around them for a moment, revealing the scene of carnage: two dead and the third twitching in his death throes. She looked down incuriously at the last of her would-be assassins and stamped down in his face, grinding her heel and pulping one eye, gouging the eye from its socket.

She laughed as she recovered her balance. "Nearly went arse over bollocks there, dearies, didn't I? Guess we should be movin' somewhere so I can have a chat and thank you and show a bit of appreciation. On the house, as it were."

"I would like that."

"Good. Maybe you and me could do some business together. I need a man—but that can wait. Let's get out of here before those shots bring some nosy bugger."

"The fog will quiet it."

"True, dearie. We'll see how I can help you when we get back to my place. Should never have come here. Knew those Chinkies were after me. Some business of a debt."

"I have nowhere to live," said Cuchillo quietly. "I have only come to this city today."

"Then you couldn't have done a favor to a better person. Straight you couldn't. My name's Magnolia Mavis Speke. Not real, of course. But when you're runnin' a good whorehouse and gamblin' rooms it sounds better than my real name."

"What is that?" asked the Apache as he took her proffered arm and they began to move away from the city in the chilly embrace of the mist.

"Miriam Poliakov. Right mouthful, eh! Come on, make haste. You've surely landed on your feet, and no mistake."

Cuchillo had never heard the expression but the meaning was plain. Though within the hour it wasn't his feet he was on.

CHAPTER EIGHT

He wasn't on his feet at all.

He was on his back, being ridden hard by Magnolia Speke, as she preferred to be called, his eyes looking over her heaving bosom at the mirrored ceiling of her own private room. Her "boudoir," she insisted.

She wasn't the most loving woman that Cuchillo had ever bedded, showing the same kind of rapid efficiency in their coupling that she'd displayed in dispatching the wounded Chinese—a thought which Cuchillo found somewhat disturbing but which he managed to subdue. Because what she lacked in tenderness she made up for in her skill and enthusiasm, tiring the Apache out with her repeated whispering and grasping and licking and sucking, constantly telling him that she wanted to show him her *full* appreciation for saving her life.

Only at four in the morning, with the sky already lightening to the east and the sounds of the city stirring about them, did she finally relax, lying back alongside the drained Apache and talking quietly about herself, and about her plans.

Magnolia had come to the West Coast eight years earlier with her mother, a redoubtable whorehouse owner. It had only taken a year or so for her to become established in the bordello, high on the north-facing slopes of one of the most fashionable hills of the city. Her mother had paid her dues and soon became exceedingly wealthy by offering clean girls at fair prices with good liquor.

"An honest whore will always get rich, Cuchillo, and my mother became very rich. I was brought up in the house of assignation." She stopped for a moment, head cradled on the pillow, a small cigar dangling from her mouth. "My mother had a friend called Hypatia Adler who was always urging her to send me away to school. 'A house is not a home for a young child,' she'd say. But I was nineteen at the time so I took scant heed of her."

"What happened to your mother?" he asked.

"Ma?"

"Yes. She still lives?"

"Lord, no! Ma got took by a fever on Christmas Day four years ago. She had been full of the seasonal spirit and a deal of port wine and attempted to entertain the entire crew of a French brigantine. Including the cabin-boy and the ni~ger cook. It was too much in chilly weather and the damp sank to her lungs. She died on the first day of the New Year."

Magnolia Speke would only talk a little about the affair with the Orientals.

"They were from the Green Window Tong, Cuchillo. I'd been 'avin' a bit of a falling-out with 'em."

"Tong? That is the secret society of the yellow men?"

"Right."

"I recall hearing word of them once. They sometimes fight with small war axes."

"Hatchets. Tuck them in their belt. Their leader came round one day and tried to persuade me to pay them some rent."

"Rent? He is the landlord?"

She reached over him, her breasts pressing into the hard wall of muscle across his stomach, stubbing out the smouldering butt of her cigar. "No. Said I'd be protected if I paid. Protected! Me!"

"You did not pay him?"

"I broke a vase over his little Chinky skull. Shoved his head in a full pisspot to bring him round and threw him out the window." Magnolia laughed delightedly at the memory. "Taught him about his 'plotection' he offered. That's what that fight was about."

"They will try again," said the warrior quietly, feeling his lust for the woman swelling yet again, touching the soft flesh under the curves of her buttocks.

"Perhaps. Mmm, that's nice. Hang on, let me roll

over a bit and . . . there." Using her left hand she guided him into her waiting deeps and he felt the warm grip as she moved her hips slowly back against him.

"What can I do?"

"Just what you're doing now. God, but you're a big bugger, Cuchillo. If you set a mind to it you could rip a girl and hurt her horrible."

For the next twenty minutes they were both too busy to carry on the conversation, tangling sweatily with each other, the crumpled sheets kicked off on the floor. There was once a tentative knock on the door, but Magnolia called out and they heard steps going away again down the corridor.

Only afterwards did they talk again, with her long black hair uncoiled across his shoulder. She was extremely tall, not far from his own six feet, and the Indian noticed how well they seemed to fit together. Her brown eyes were nearly closed and she seemed to be almost asleep as she spoke to him, her voice coming and going like the far-off, half-heard sound of water.

"Man like you, Cuchillo . . . hell of a man. I've been waiting a long time for someone I could maybe think about taking into the business here."

"To do what?"

"Look after things." She leaned up and kissed him hard on the lips. "Look after me, love. You're good at that. Best I've known."

"Protect you?"

"That as well. But not just like that. Like a partner. In a year or so I'm hopin' to get some dollars together and buy the place next door. Knock it through and run it as part of the business. Do food there. Dancing. Orchestra. Give us top class."

"You need money?"

"Round 'bout fifteen thousand dollars would do it. Why?" She laughed softly, stretching her magnificent body like a great cat. "You offerin' me?"

Cuchillo nodded. "If we are partners . . . that was your word?"

"Sure."

"Then I would have a share?"

She sat up suddenly, pulling the sheets up around her breasts, and he sensed the change in her attitude. What had gone before had been pleasure. Now came the business, and again he felt the hardness in the woman that had kept her alive and successful in a city of wolves.

"You joshin' me. Indian?"

"No. You said you wanted me to be with you."

"Sure, but I meant as a kind of friend and strongarm man. I'd have paid you."

"You said partners."

"I didn't . . . Let me try and understand you, Cuchillo. Plain speaking now."

She had undressed in a small anteroom, and he had been careful not to let her see the money-belt, hiding it beneath his shirt. And he had said nothing about his adventures during the previous months. Nor had he mentioned the vengeful Thaddeus Mann.

"You said you need fifteen thousand dollars to

make your house bigger. If I give you this, then you will make me partner?"

"Just a minute, mister. I'm not gettin' involved with stolen gold. What is it? Cavalry payroll?"

"It is mine," he replied angrily.

"Where the hell does . . . ?" Then she stopped, hand going to protect her face from the raised fist, seeing the mask of bright anger behind it.

"No," he whispered, dropping his hand, slowly allowing the tense fingers to uncoil. "I will not hit you."

"I'm sorry, Cuchillo. Real sorry. I didn't think what I . . ."

"That is . . . You would have asked where a naked savage can find so much dollars. I do not have fifteen thousand. But I have nearly fourteen. Here," leaning from the high bed and flourishing the belt at her. "Nearly fourteen thousand dollars in American money."

Magnolia Spéke kept silent. Like any really good whore she knew that there was a time to talk and a time to remain mute.

"You ask how I can have this. It is mine. Given by a friend. A white man, murdered by another white man. And I would give this all to you so that we might be partners. But you do not trust me."

"Hey, quiet down. You'll wake the whole damned house up." Cuchillo Oro did not even realize that he had raised his voice in his temper and he lay back once more while she stroked his chest. "You got the finest body I ever did see, but it's kind of odd on a big man like you seeing no hair on your chest. No beard, neither."

"My people are not made in that manner."

"Listen, Chuchillo. I'm sorry. It was a foolish thing to say to you. I'm truly sorry."

So he told her. Before breakfast, brought up by a giggling maid: fine ham and eggs served with a great side dish of potatoes, shredded and fried, with a silver pot of coffee. All the time that they ate he told her about himself, finding an ease he could never recall with any other woman. With any other person, apart from John Hedges.

She listened to him, occasionally nodding, or murmuring a question. The whole tale of his early life, marriage and his baby. The night of slaughter by the blue-bellies and the seemingly endless feud with Pinner. Then he talked about Sheriff Thaddeus Mann and the happenings in One Hundred Year Gulch.

"He'll try and follow you here?"

"No."

"You said . . ."

"Not *try*."

"You figure he's good enough to track you all the way here? This is a big city, Cuchillo Oro. Thousands of folks here."

"The forests are full of trees, but I could track a man there however far he ran. This sheriff will do the same to me. One day. Tomorrow. Next year. Some time. Mann is good enough."

"Better than you?"

The Apache considered the question for some time, weighing his answer. "Perhaps not. But I do not wish to stake my life on the difference."

"You was friends when you last saw him?"

"Yes. But I think that the next time he will be more careful. More cold. I have seen anger eat into the heart of a man until he lived only for it. I know that as well as any man. He knows it and I saw things in his eyes that were like madness. There will be no more friendliness, I think."

Eventually, a little before noon, Magnolia Speke agreed that she would take the Apache warrior on as her partner. Taking his thirteen thousand, eight hundred and forty dollars and using it to purchase the property next door to her bordello. Arranging with her lawyer to draw up a document making Cuchillo the half-owner of the whole deal.

"Now you can get yourself civilized, dear," she said to him as they lay together in her bed a few nights later.

It was an idea that had always appealed to the lone Indian. To wear good clothes and eat well. No longer to have to fight and kill simply to survive in the jungle of the western frontier.

And now that lay within his grasp.

That night he slept well, secure for the first time in many years, feeling instinctively that this time it was all going to work out well.

CHAPTER NINE

Late summer in San Francisco, with the evening mists carrying a touch more dampness and cold in their soft embrace.

Up at the renamed Lucky Miner restaurant, gambling rooms, saloon and brothel, it was business as usual. A crowd of the wealthy and fashionable of the city came to the Lucky Miner from their own elevated houses, so that they might see and be seen in the most elegant spot on the Bay.

Magnolia Speke was moving from room to room, supremely stylish in a gown of dark blue silk, shot through with panels of lighter blue, her black hair coiled up under a tasteful and expensive tiara, topped with a cluster of tiny emeralds. She wore a massive fan of lilac ostrich feathers on her right wrist. As she walked through her empire she nodded to those she favored, exchanging a word here and there with the leaders of San Francisco.

Always close by, sometimes shadowing her steps and sometimes preceding her, came the silent figure of a very tall, swarthy man dressed in a dark suit of costly cut, with highly polished boots, and a silk cravat pinned in place with a gold pin, the star pattern of emeralds matching those of his lover's tiara. Cuchillo's thick hair was trimmed to his shoulders and he had bunched it up at the back, tucking it into a black, low-crowned hat.

Nobody ever mentioned openly the fact that Magnolia's partner was a full-blooded Apache warrior who had personally killed a good many whites. Yet it was a subject of gossip, lustful among the men and more brazenly sensual among the chattering wives. How often did they . . . ? Did she really let him . . . ? Was it true that he was even better endowed than the big buck nigra who sometimes exhibited himself down at . . . ?

Magnolia was genuinely very fond of Cuchillo, and in the privacy of her own mind in the waking hours of the early morning she would even admit to being in love with him. But she was shrewd enough to know that at least part of her newly increased success came from her pairing with the Indian. And on his part Cuchillo was also fully aware of his own curiosity value and exploited it by being even more silent and menacing than usual.

Locked away in a small room at the back of his skull was the other awareness, that this attractive white woman loved him, and that he . . . He didn't know. He liked her. Liked her to a point where his real happiness each day came in the early hours after midnight when the Lucky Miner was closed and everyone had gone home and he and Magnolia could tumble wearily into each other's arms.

The conflict in his mind came not from his deepening relationship with Magnolia. It lay in his tribal roots, with the knowledge that he had achieved the ambition of many Indians. They admired and feared the white men, and some were eager to live among them as equals and learn their skills and ways. To pass for white was something that virtually none of them had the faintest hope of ever achieving, and yet he'd done it. Wearing white clothes and eating white food. Sleeping in a luxurious bed with a stunningly attractive white woman. He'd been lucky enough to make his money in a rough mining camp where there was little prejudice against a man because of his background. And now, in cosmopolitan San Francisco he was accepted in the same way, mixing with the leaders of society.

There had been a few moments of trouble when they had just opened the annex to the Lucky Miner and some local residents had complained about having "that naked heathen" as a neighbor. The police chief had called around and tried to lean a little on Cuchillo, who had responded by throwing him neck and crop down the main stairs. The man had drawn a gun and only the intervention of Magnolia in her full pomp and wrath had stopped a killing. The police officer had threatened to come back with a posse and take Cuchillo out and hang him from a pole. Magnolia had sent half a dozen of her girls out, in their demure Sunday best, with messages for some of their more influential clients.

They never heard any more about the police chief and the problem disappeared.

"I'm lookin' forward to this play, Cuchillo, my darling."

"I do not like theatres."

"Why?" She pulled a face at him in her mirror.

"Men and women pretending to be what they are not. It is not true."

Magnolia turned round and stuck out her tongue. "You ignorant savage, you! If you want to be anything in decent society, you great bear, then you must do what is right and proper."

She was wearing only a thin shift and he walked over and stood behind her as she gazed at herself in the glass, pursing her lips as she applied her makeup. He reached over the white shoulder and let his hand drop to cup her full breast, making her sigh and wriggle in the seat.

"Leave me, please. I'll be late if we tumble off and get swivin' again. I know. Once isn't enough and twice is just for a beginning."

He stepped back and walked to the window, tugging back the lace curtain, looking out over the foggy city, watching an elegant landau roll past, its liveried driver flicking at the horses with a long whip.

"What is this play called?"

"Just a moment. Ah, can you help hook me in, dear man? Thank you."

"The play?"

"Are you goin' to wear that new signet ring I bought you, Cuchillo?"

"Yes."

"Unless it is too tight, but . . . And the gold hunter, dearest. It is the finest timepiece in all of San Francisco, they say."

"I have it in my coat here." Though he hadn't mentioned it to Magnolia, Cuchillo had virtually forgotten how to tell time and he had been forced to ask other people in roundabout ways, to check his memory.

"Good. I swear you must be the most handsome man and the audience . . . the women in the audience will all swoon at the sight of you and envy me my fine lover."

"But what is the name of the play that we must go and watch?"

She was bustling about their room, searching for her reticule, and her mind was only partly on his repeated question.

"Mmmm? What's that?"

Cuchillo was becoming angered. "I asked what—" he began.

"Oh, the play. It is called *Our American Cousin*. Most droll, they say. Of course, you know that it was the very play that our poor dear President Lincoln was watching when he—Who's there?"

It was the maid with the news that their carriage was ready for them. And so Cuchillo never did get to hear what happened to President Lincoln while he had been enjoying *Our American Cousin*.

The theatre was packed for the eagerly awaited visit to the city of the renowned dramatic company who had traveled clean across the country from New York to present their entertainment. The building smelled of fine cigars and good perfume and the air was abuzz with excited chatter, rising above the hissing of the stage lights.

Magnolia had used her influence to obtain a box for herself and Cuchillo, to the right of the stage, in one of a bank of six, matched by six more shadowed caves on the opposite side. The lighting from the body of the theatre didn't reach into the boxes and each one was a dim pool of mystery, with only an occasional gloved hand or the flash of gold off the lenses of a pair of eyeglasses to betray their occupants.

For Cuchillo Oro it should have been one of the highest moments of his life. He had made it in the world of the white man, his way eased by the silvered oil of thousands of dollars, smoothed further by the influential contacts of a rich madam.

There he was, in the most fashionable of clothes, through he admitted to himself that he would have been far more comfortable in his old breeches and cotton shirt. Much as the Apache had wanted to continue wearing his golden knife, Magnolia had stopped him, saying that it would spoil the cut of his vest. And besides, elegant people did not take their weapons when going out for an evening at the theatre.

He'd enjoyed a good meal and a glass of genuine French wine, imported clear from Paris. But it lay heavy on his stomach, filling him so that it seemed as though the rich pastries and meats hung chokingly at the back of his throat.

It was an odd contrast for him, from the slow dying of the township of Thaddeus Mann to the fast living of San Francisco. Though he kept trying to convince himself that he was happy, and that was the way he wanted to live, Cuchillo was far from certain.

And the company!

It was unthinkable that he, a penniless warrior from the poor tribe of the Mimbrenos Apaches of southwest Arizona, should be mingling with men who counted their fortunes in millions of dollars, and whose houses employed more servants than there were fighting men in Cuchillo's tribe. That very evening they'd pressed around him, shaking his hand and asking him about the fights he'd had with the soldiers, some of them paying court to Magnolia Speke, knowing that her girls held secrets that could wreck their ambitions and families. There are few more powerful women than those who run brothels catering for the rich and famous.

The lights dimmed and the chattering gradually hushed. The red plush curtain swished upwards in a whisper of ponderous movement and the bright lights on the stage flared out.

The play had begun.

Cuchillo had decided that if there was such a thing as love, then it might be that he was beginning to be in love with Magnolia Speke. She was the sort of woman that had always attracted him: tall and strong, fearless and independent, loyal to her friends and scathing toward her enemies. But that wasn't enough. The lovemaking was better than anything he could have imagined, and she had introduced him to ideas he had never known, led him down paths he had no concept even existed. But that wasn't enough.

The life was already jading, palling on him with its easy success and effortless luxury. That wasn't what he truly wanted. But he was becoming like a plump spider caught in its own silken web, struggling less and less against the soft cords.

If only he and Magnolia could have moved away from the city. Perhaps they could sell up and use the profits to buy a spread somewhere. Maybe someplace like Oregon, or even Canada, where not too many questions would be asked about a white woman and a full-blooded Apache.

Perhaps.

Christian Walker Collingwood was playing the part of the wealthy merchant, Asa Trenchard, trying to avoid the attentions of the social climber, Mrs.

Mount-Chessington, played by Evangeline Spencer, who was trying to force the hand of her daughter, played with great charm by the young Lorraine Stotter.

Cuchillo Oro was not enjoying the play, finding the wordy jokes hard to follow, contenting himself with watching the actress playing the daughter, occasionally leaning forward over the padded edge of the box to stare down at the audience. Once he borrowed the glasses from Magnolia and let his eyes range around the theatre, shaking his head in puzzlement at the array of dusty golden cherubs that decorated the ceiling corners.

The other boxes interested him and he focused on the half-dozen opposite, smiling a little as the light from the stage caught the pale hand of a moustachio'd gallant delving deep in the bosom of his young companion while her mother, or aunt, sat oblivious at the near side of the box.

"What are you looking at?" hissed Magnolia Speke, aware that her companion had lost interest in the merry happenings behind the lights.

"I watch the people watch the play."

"Why not watch the play instead?"

"I do not like it."

"Oh, Cuchillo, you must learn to enjoy things like this if we are ever to get on in decent society."

And she turned her back on him with a sniff of disapproval, making him even more intent that he would talk to her in bed that very night about the possibility of their leaving San Francisco some time before the next summer and trying life together in a way that would not make him feel stifled at every moment.

He again allowed the glasses to roam across the dark face of the theatre, finding that they brought an odd sense of unreality to what he watched. The lenses brought everything closer, and yet it was silent. The words from the stage drummed at his ears and yet he could clearly see the lips of the young man moving as he whispered to his companion.

There was a brief gleam of light in the box almost opposite as if the door at the back had been rapidly opened and closed.

"Here comes a good bit," whispered Magnolia, without turning her head. "Hypatia Whitehead told me of it. She saw this play when she was in New Orleans last fall."

The Indian leaned forward, still holding the binoculars, noticing out of the corner of his eye that there had been a quick flash of reflected light from the box opposite, almost as though someone was watching him through glasses. Since San Francisco society was notoriously inquisitive, it didn't surprise him in the least. Though it did just stir a feather of disquiet at the back of his mind. A feeling that he quickly shrugged off, seeing Magnolia's happy face in profile, wrapped in the drama on the stage below them.

Over the weeks with her, Cuchillo had come to know a lot about Magnolia Speke, born Miriam Poliakov. Her father had changed his name to Polly, or had been given the changed name by one of the stone-faced immigration officials when he landed in America from Europe. He'd been a draper and had failed to come to terms with the new lands. Then he had died in a fire—an accident, they claimed, despite the razor gripped tight in his hand—and Miriam's mother had first opened a tea shop, only later going into a far more profitable line of buisness.

The Indian kept glancing at his woman. Magnolia didn't talk much about her father, except to laugh about his habit of avoiding debtors by looking out of the shop window and rushing out and vanishing, muttering "Little dog," as he went.

Christian Walker Collingwood was staring up into the darkness of the theatre while Mrs. Mount-Chessington berated him in a piercing voice. The shrillness dragged Cuchillo's mind back to the play.

"I am aware, dear Mr. Trenchard, that you are not used to the manners of good society and that alone will excuse the impertinence of which you have been guilty!"

With that she swept off the stage, her gown rustling across the floor, while the audience shifted in their seats, bursting with anticipation for the line that they knew came next.

Collingwood had moved further to the side of the stage and Magnolia craned her neck, trying to see him, tapping Cuchillo urgently on the arm.

"What is it?"

"Change seats. Quickly! I couldn't bear to miss this. Quickly!"

With an imperceptible movement Cuchillo slipped sideways behind her and took her seat while she leaned out from his padded chair, clasping her hands in front of her in excitement. The change was done so quickly that not a single person in the theatre saw it. There were still the two silhouetted figures in the box, just as there had been when the house lights were dimmed.

Collingwood began to speak. "Don't know the manners of decent society, eh? Well, I . . ." He paused as the laughter swelled, mentally cursing the fact that his best line was now so well known that audiences laughed at it in advance. But he smiled and bowed slight, waiting a moment.

"Oh, go on," whispered Magnolia Speke.

"Well, I guess that I know enough to turn you inside-out, old gel. You sockdologising old mantrap!"

It never failed.

The theatre rocked with the laughter and delighted applause, the sound filling and becoming deafening, every eye turned to the stage and every ear dulled by the noise.

So that nobody even heard the sound of Thaddeus Mann's rifle as he fired at the shadow he knew to be Cuchillo Oro, just visible in the box opposite. He saw the jolt as the bullet hit home and the figure disappeared. For the first time in many months, the aging lawman felt happy.

CHAPTER TEN

The reactions of Cuchillo Oro were far faster than any white man, yet even he couldn't believe what had happened. His mind refused to admit that there had been a shot, yet he knew it was so. And he immediately knew who had done it and why. There was a momentary flicker of doubt that it might have been one of their enemies in the city, perhaps the Chinese again. But such a killing wasn't their way.

"Mann," he said, between clenched teeth.

He hadn't heard the sound of the gun, but the muzzle flash had caught his eyes, his mind dismissing it as someone lighting a cigar with a lucifer. But the reaction of the woman at his side was unmistakable. Magnolia jerked back in her chair, arms flying outwards, then she slumped down, sliding to the floor of the dark box. The Apache had caught the hatchet blow sound of the bullet hitting her in the head, and had felt the warm spray of blood and brains in his own face.

He dropped to his knees, cradling her in his arms, hearing the breath sighing from her open mouth.

"Magnolia! Magnolia!"

But it was too late. By changing seats they had thrown off the assassin and she was dying instead of him.

Dead.

In the blackness Cuchillo couldn't even see the entrance wound, but he touched her, feeling the great splash of blood above the right eye, her hair tumbling loose and the shattered skull soft and pulped against the support of his right hand.

All around them the audience still roared and cheered, while Christian Collingwood bowed and waved a hand to acknowledge their reception. But Cuchillo Oro saw and heard none of it. He was locked in his own black purgatory, cuddling the corpse of the woman he had loved.

Once he kissed her.

Once only, tasting her blood on his lips.

Then he laid her down in the dusty darkness, standing over the body, left hand instinctively reaching for the golden knife, lips taut off his white teeth in a snarl of animal anger. Anger that deepened as he realised that his weapons were back at the Lucky Miner and that he stood there, sporting all the trappings of the white man's civilization, helpless to go after the killer.

"Soon, Thaddeus Mann. By all my gods, it will be soon."

It took him twenty-five minutes to get back to the brothel, fighting a desperate battle with himself to keep self-control. Steadying his breathing and forcing himself to step quietly from the box, closing the door firmly behind him without a backwards glance. Walking along the deserted corridor and out of the theatre into the bustling streets of the city.

He tried to run but the fog had made the streets slippery and the hand-made, fifty-dollar shoes were tight across the width of his feet and pinched him. Once he fell, sliding into the gutter, smearing his suit with horse droppings, bursting the seam on the left arm. His hat came off and his long hair unrolled itself and blew about his broad shoulders.

Once he lost his way and found himself in a narrow alley, lined with empty barrels. There was a man there, humping against a raddled whore, her skirt up around her waist, her face staring blankly over his shoulders. The man heard Cuchillo's steps and pulled himself away, his penis instantly limp, pressing himself back against one of the slimy walls.

"Please, mister . . . don't . . ." he said, but Cuchillo had already turned and gone on, his eyes registering everything he saw, but his mind blanking out on everything except the memory of the softness of his woman's skull and the warmth of her blood.

The brothel was doing its usual business as he ran up the main steps. The bouncers at the front door saw him coming and both stepped out to stop him, not recognizing the dishevelled, long-haired figure as their employer.

Cuchillo paused a moment, ready to kill them

both with his bare hands, but one of them finally saw who it was and they stepped aside, letting him through.

"Good evening, Mr.—My God!" exclaimed the English butler whom Magnolia had employed to give an even greater touch of class to her enterprise.

In the bright lights of the hall everyone could see what a dreadful sight Cuchillo Oro was. Drying blood was congealed all across his face and hands, dappling the lace frills of his shirt. His clothes were wet and stained, his shoes splattered with mud. The hat was gone and his hair framed a face almost inhuman in its blind mixture of anger and desolation.

The crowds of diners and gamblers parted in front of him like the Red Sea at Moses' command, letting him stalk through, watching in silence as he vanished up the grand stairs towards their private suite of rooms. Now it was his suite alone.

The Indian disappeared and slammed the door shut behind him, and the frightened staff waited huddled outside, hearing what sounded like a bitter fight in the room.

But Cuchillo was alone.

That thought penetrated his rage and he took it out on the superficial trapping of the whites. Ripping his jacket off, tearing it to shreds with his strong hands. Pulling off the gold hunter watch and throwing it as hard as he could against the wall, deriving a grim pleasure from the satisfactory way it smashed, glass and springs and tiny cogwheels flying everywhere.

He knew that it could only be a matter of minutes before the authorities discovered Magnolia's body in the theatre and they would quickly be around, and again he would be a hunted man. There would be long explanations, but they would only work with men prepared to listen. What he must do was flee, fast and far.

It took him only moments to strip himself completely naked, leaving his jewels on the floor, so that he could dress himself again in the clothes of an Apache warrior. Arming himself with his beloved knife and sticking the Navy Colt he had bought in his belt. Tying a length of colored material about his hair to bind it back from his forehead. Not even noticing that it was one of Magnolia's scarves that he had taken.

He looked a last time around the room, hearing the music and laughter from downstairs where life went on. It barely crossed his mind that all of that belonged to him. At that moment of frozen time after Mann's bullet had ripped the life from Magnolia Speke, Cuchillo Oro was probably the richest Apache in history. He stood there the undoubted owner of the entire operation, worth at least a hundred thousand dollars.

There were two ornamental oil lamps, brass with Corinthian columns, fluted and immeasurably elegant and stylish. They filled the bedroom with their warm, golden glow, and for some reason the sight of their comforting light brought Cuchillo from a seething anger to one of the dangerous blind rages that he had thought long under control.

He lashed out with his crippled right hand, knocking the nearest lamp to the floor. Oil spilled across the patterned carpet. The flame smoked and the tiny yellow light suddenly flared, the dark oil igniting across the room.

The sight brought a bizarre comfort to Cuchillo. Since his attempt to live as a white man had failed and ended in tragedy, then he would destroy it all. The house was his. Magnolia had said so and there had been papers, with his own jagged, crabbed signature at their bottom. The restaurant was his. The saloon and all the liquor. The bordello and every single bed and sheet.

"All mine," he grunted, hefting the second lamp and throwing it toward the bed. The glass hit the carved panel at the head of the double bed, splintering, blazing oil spreading immediately, igniting the coverlet. Racing like virulent red snakes, the flames spread across the floor, catching the drapes and furniture.

"All mine."

He went around the room smashing every item of glass or china, snatching great armfuls of dresses from the wardrobes, heaving them on the yellow fire, filling the room with thick smoke.

"Mine."

Before he left the chamber Cuchillo broke the

high window, allowing cool night air to rush in and feed the inferno. He unlocked the door and opened it suddenly, finding himself at the middle of a crowd of nervous, chattering servants, who recoiled from the dreadful sight of the huge, savage Apache, wreathed about with smoke and fire.

It was the butler who had sufficient control and nerve to speak. "Will there be anything that you require, sir? Water to extinguish the flames?"

The Indian shook his head. The mind-turning rage had eased and all he sought now was revenge on Thaddeus Mann. He tried even at that moment to guess where the old man would have gone. Not west. Not north with winter coming.

"South," he said.

"I beg your pardon, Mr. Oro? What was that you said, sir?"

"You must go. All of you. Everyone. It is finished and your mistress dead."

He ignored their wide-eyed shock, stalking down the stairs, out of the building, collecting a horse from the stables. Riding through the city, towards the south. And no man dared to try to check him. Cuchillo Oro stopped only once, looking back across the sharp-edged buildings toward the Lucky Miner, now totally and hopelessly ablaze, whirling pillars of red sparks setting fire already to neighboring buildings.

"It was mine," he muttered, and didn't look back again.

CHAPTER ELEVEN

"Old man?"

Cuchillo nodded, patiently holding the bridle of his bay gelding while it drank thirstily from the tree-fringed pool.

"Greying hair. Tall. Meaner than a cornered rattler. That him?"

Again Cuchillo nodded, feeling satisfaction that his skill at second-guessing Mann hadn't deserted him. The lawman had chosen to go south.

"Two others with him."

"What?"

The homesteader took a nasty step back at the flaring anger in the Indian's voice, wishing that he hadn't left his brass-bound Spencer on the porch, fifty paces off, but glad that his wife and teenage daughter were up on the north forty, out of sight of this menacing Apache. There hadn't been Indian trouble in those parts for more years than he could remember, but that wouldn't stop a lone renegade from having his way.

"Sure. Sure, mister. Two of 'em."

"What were they like?"

"Mean. One around twenty, carryin' a Dragoon, tied real low on his leg. The other nearer forty. Hair redder than blood."

"They were together?"

"Sure were. But not like friends. Seemed the old man—the one interests you—kind of was the boss hand with 'em."

"Did they use names?"

"Yeah. Kid was called Mario."

"Maria? That is a woman's name."

The little man shook his head, feeling relief that the anger had passed on. It was clear that this big buck was only concerned about his pursuit. And from the iron in his eyes, it would be a hard meeting.

"Mario. With an O at the end. I guess it's foreign. French or somethin' like. Yellow sort of skin. Sweated a lot. Black hair. My daughter took . . ." He hesitated, realizing his nervous tongue was running away. But Cuchillo was showing no special interest in the mention of his girl. "She liked him," he finished lamely.

The Apache pulled his thoughts back to the men. "The others?"

"What?"

"Names?"

"The other was called red. Hair like that and you couldn't rightly think of nothin' else."

"I thank you for the water," said Cuchillo Oro.

"I could give you some corn dodgers, mister. We

don't have a lot. Hard times out here. Last year the rivers swelled. Flash floods washed us out. Brought us close to the grave and that's the truth."

"The old man. Did they call him by any name? Mr. Mann? Thaddeus?"

"Hey. That's my name, Mister, you know. Thaddeus Tanner." He wiped a hand back over his thinning hair and beamed. "What they calls a coincidence, that."

"Was his name that?"

"No. Well, I don't rightly know. The other two didn't talk much to him. Seemed a mite scared. The kid called him Sheriff once."

"Yes." A long sigh. "That is him. And they left here how long?"

"Not more than . . ." squinting at the sun, "three hours. Pushed on fast south and west. Toward the sea. Sure about them dodgers?"

"No."

"Nothin' more I can do for you?"

"No. I thank you for your help. If I could pay you I would."

"You goin' to kill them three?"

"I will try."

In the dipping streets of San Francisco Thaddeus Mann would have held all of the aces, his urban skills giving him an edge over the Indian. Surrounded by buildings and crowds, much of Cuchillo's wood-wise crafts would have been useless. And that miscalculation seemed a sign that Mann's obsession to kill Cuchillo had tipped his judgment.

The Indian had figured that the old lawman would have waited just long enough to see the corpse of his enemy. And once he realized that he had shot the wrong person he would see the need to run. That could be why he had seemingly taken on a couple of other guns. That too was a sign of a change in the sheriff. The man that Cuchillo had first met would never have considered he needed help to kill one man.

And Thaddeus Tanner had mentioned, while the horse drank its fill, that the old man had seemed kind of odd. What had he said about him? Cuchillo wrinkled his forehead to recall the words.

"Looked like a man touched by the sun. Mutterin' to hisself. Heard him say about a dead town. That don't make sense, does it? Someone had killed a town. And there was a woman's name. Rachel. That was it. Said he'd see her again soon. Must be his woman."

Cuchillo wondered if the lawman had gone mad. He'd seen it before: pressures building up so that everything normal became odd and the bizarre became commonplace. Cyrus Pinner had become like that, any goodness in him squeezed out like the juice from an orange, replaced by a crazed evil.

There was only a few hours to go to sunset. The trial forked beyond the homestead. Tanner had said that they had gone westwards, towards the sea. Mann would know that the Apache would likely be closing after them. That was the reason for the other two men. It crossed Cuchillo's mind that the lawman might have bribed or threatened the little farmer to mislead him, but he dismissed the idea.

At the fork he paused, getting off his horse to kneel and examine the tracks. Three horses, heading for the cooler-tasting air from the coast. It had been a long time since Cuchillo had last seen the sea and he tested his memory, wondering it if had truly been as large as he recalled. The touch of fear at the remembered vastness was enough.

He set heels to his horse and began to canter slowly towards the setting sun, feeling calmer and better than for some time. The situation was under his control, and this time it would finish.

One way or the other, it would finish.

He killed the kid, Mario, just before evening on the following day.

It was easy.

The three of them had camped in a draw about eleven miles from the sea, near enough for a chill mist to creep in on grey-tendriled fingers among the stark trees as the sun dipped over the last range of hills to the west of them. Mann sat back against a big old cypress, hat tugged down over his eyes. The red-haired man started a fire, sending Mario for water.

Cuchillo regretted that he hadn't brought a long gun with him, as it might have been possible to kill Mann from cover with a single shot. But he knew his own limitations with a rifle and a miss would have been a potentially fatal mistake.

There was a steep-sided canyon about two hundred yards from the campsite, with foaming water bursting from a cleft among the rocks, tumbling down a vertical wall of glittering stone into a deep pool. There was a faint trail from the camp to the top of the fall, then cutting down the side of the cliff.

It was near there that Cuchillo Oro waited for the young boy with the foreign name, and killed him.

Mario was seventeen, eager to make a lot of money so that he could send it home to his small village in northern Sicily and bring the rest of his family over. His father was dead, victim of a shotgun blast that been a minor punctuation mark in a major feud that had decimated the male side of Mario's family for generations. So he was the oldest son, and it had been a great sacrifice for them all to scrape together the dollars to send him to the new land. And if he failed them, then his mother and five sisters and three younger brothers would be condemned for all their lives to grinding penury that stopped only fractionally on the right side of starvation. It was a heavy responsibility but one that he bore like the man he thought himself.

He had met up with Red after an abortive attempt to steal money from a store in a township in the foothills of the Sierras. Mario hadn't even known the name of the place. The old woman behind the counter had grabbed at him instead of being frightened of the gaping muzzle of the Dragoon, pulling his long hair and screaming for help. Red had been in there buying himself some shells and had calmly taken a hand-axe from the counter and buried it in the back of the woman's skull, with a thunk like splitting kindling.

Since then they'd been together, and had been ready to roll some drunk for small change in San Francisco when they'd met Thaddeus Mann. The old sheriff was clearly not right in the head and talked only of his dead wife and his dead settlement. It seemed from the mutterings of the grey-haired shootist that he believed a giant Apache had been responsible for both happenings. He said that the Indian would come after them.

Neither Mario nor Red really believed in the existence of this Cuchillo Oro. Mario had come straight west from New Jersey and Red was from Chicago. Neither had spent any time further south than San Francisco, and had scarcely even seen a friendly Indian, never mind a hostile Apache.

But Mann was paying them well to stay with him, and money was what counted. They'd agreed that they'd go with him for another two days, just to make sure he trusted them. Then they'd kill him and take his roll.

So Mario wasn't that worried about any enemies when he carried the canteens along the rocky trail, starting to pick his way down the slippery path towards the still pool.

He walked round a corner, pressing himself as

flat as he could against the wall of stone, trying not to get moss on his only clean shirt. The roar of the water drowned out all sounds.

The boy was whistling to himself, head turned to look at the tumbling wall of green-white water. Cuchillo reached out from a crevice in the stone, locking his mutilated right hand about his neck, sticking the golden knife hard under the left shoulder, twisting it as he withdrew it. The kid dropped to his knees, hands pressed to his chest, the empty canteens falling and bouncing into the water below.

The Apache, on an impulse of anger, gripped him from behind, by the hair, sawing the razored steel across the throat, through the bubbling windpipe, all the way round until it grated on the spine. Then he kicked the bloodied corpse in the back so that it flopped once on a protruding rock and then fell into the deep pool, hanging face down in the water, the current carrying it towards a low beach, looking from above like a child playing at being a starfish.

Mario never knew what had happened. He didn't know if he screamed, the thunder of the waterfall filling his ears. There was the man seizing him, but he never saw who it was, and then the blow. His eyes were already fading when Cuchillo slit his throat as if he were slaughtering a captive hog, and there was little pain to his passing. Not even time for regret for his family doomed to endless misery back home in Sicily.

* * *

It was a half hour before Thaddeus Mann missed the boy. He sat up quickly, hand reaching for the butt of his pistol, shaking his head as if he were trying to clear away cobwebs. Nowadays it seemed harder for him to think clearly, more difficult to plan and act with any kind of determination.

"Where's the boy?"

"What?" The big man, Red, was dozing on the far side of the clearing, the sun hot on the front of his trousers, rousing him to an erection. But he was too tired to do much about it, contenting himself with unbuttoning and slipping a hand inside to caress himself sleepily, thinking about a young boy he'd laid up in Denver. A grin crept across the ginger stubble on his cheeks as he recalled how the kid had screamed and fought as he'd penetrated him.

"The boy?"

"Huh? The one up in Denver? I don't recall saying anythin' 'bout that, Sheriff."

"No, you damned fool! Mario. He's been gone too long just for water."

"How long?" He did up the front of his pants and stood up. He carried a big Walker pistol and he drew it, cocking back on the heavy action with effortless strength.

"Thirty, forty minutes. Let's go."

God damn it to hell." Red was going to be very upset if anything had happened to the dark-skinned, cat-eyed youth. Though he hadn't yet made any obvious advances towards him, the slender waist and tight hips had disturbed his sleep a few times since they'd teamed up.

By the time they followed the tracks to the top of the fall, the corpse had drifted to the edge of the water, lying face down, the legs moving gently in the current of the stream.

"There," said Mann.

"Must have fallen," Red suggested, starting along the same rocky trail that Mario had followed, picking his way cautiously pistol in hand. "No sign of anyone else here, Sheriff," he shouted.

"He's around. Boy don't fall like that. Kid was careful."

"You figure this Apache of yours has caught us up, huh?"

Mann nodded, looking for another way down to the pebbled beach, climbing across the face of the boulders, spreading himself like a spider to hang on. The sun bounced off the water and silhouetted him and Cuchillo, much higher up, again regretted that he hadn't brought a rifle with him.

The two men reached the corpse together, stared down at it. The long hair fronded out from the kid's skull, water trickling from it. Mann spat in the pool.

"Told you the Indian was good. Too good for a snot-nose boy. Too good for a drunk shootist like you, Red. Maybe even too good for me."

The other man didn't reply, wishing that he and Mario had taken the old man sooner. Now it was too late for the boy. But not too late for him. Maybe the next evening? He knew Mann had a roll with him. Red could go south. Tijuana, somewhere like that. All the young boys . . .

"Sure he was murdered? Didn't hear no shot."

"Cuchillo would have strangled him. Broke his neck. Maybe used the big golden knife."

"Maybe he fell," insisted Red stubbornly, his angry voice floating up above the sound of the water, reaching the hiding Indian.

"No."

"How come you're so certain?"

"Roll him over, Red."

"I didn't, you—"

"Just do it," repeated Mann, voice dangerously calm, the barrel of his handgun seeming to move towards the big man under its own volition. "Come on, Red. I seen you lookin' at the boy often enough when he was livin'. Take a last look."

Red bent down and tugged at the kid's head, locking his fingers in the tangled hair, pulling. He staggered back with a loud gasp of horror. "Jesus!"

"Now you think he fell?"

As Red had tugged on the hair, the entire head had kind of folded back. The throat had been so comprehensively slit by Cuchillo that even the spine had gone, the bones of the neck parted by the keen-edged blade. The boy's head folded over, right against the back of the wet shirt, the dead eyes staring blank and empty at the sky. The skull was connected to the trunk only by a narrow strip of skin and gristle.

"Poor bastard. That fuckin' Indian! Where the hell is he?"

Mann stood, looking warily around the pool, seeing the bowl of green about them. His pistol probed at the trees and his hat was pushed back off his grey hair. To Chuchillo the ex-lawman looked suddenly old.

"He'll be watchin' us from up there. Don't have a long gun, do you, son?" he shouted, the echoes disturbing birds from the branches around, sending them screeching into the stillness. "You'd have done for us all if'n you had. You know I'm sorry about the woman, Cuchillo. Wasn't what I intended. Guess you know that too."

"Let's get out of here!" said the other man, wiping sweat from his temples, his bright hair flaring in the sun like a beacon fire.

"Getting scared, Red?" mocked Thaddeus Mann.

"No."

"Sure you aren't."

"You old bastard! You're crazy."

"Could be," replied Mann, so softly that Cuchillo could hardly hear him. "Folks been sayin' that for long years, Red. Long, long, empty, wasted years."

"I'm goin'."

"Take care he's not by the horses, Red."

"What?"

"Or among the rocks."

"Fuck you!" spat Red, starting to climb the path above the waterfall, taking each step as cautiously as if he were walking barefoot among scorpions.

"Or behind every tree, Red. You take care now, you hear me?"

"Fuck you, Mann." Raising his voice. "And fuck you, Cuchillo Gold-Knife!"

"Words come cheap," replied the Apache, knowing that the forest would distort his voice, making it impossible to locate. "Bullets cost dollars."

"Jesus. He's here," hissed Red, but Thaddeus Mann just laughed. And laughed.

And laughed.

CHAPTER TWELVE

Neither Mann nor Red slept much that night.

They'd ridden together, linked by mutual dislike, the shootist sticking with the elderly lawman through fear of this mysterious Indian who could come and pluck life without a sound or a sign. Red wasn't a frontier boy, used to reading the clouds and the scents of the wind. His power came in confined space, when he could use his strength to best advantage, or in dark alleys where the knife in the back or the bullet through the spine would bring their own easy reward.

Cuchillo had let them go for an hour, finding a high place where he could watch. He saw the column of dust from the two men as it spiraled into the air, and followed it with his eyes as it hung like a pointing finger, showing him Mann and Red going west, straight toward the sea. They wanted to be out of trees and steep valleys where an ambush was the easiest thing in the world. Thaddeus Mann was

115

trying to find somewhere safe to hole up so that the Apache would have to come at him from a weaker position.

"Cuchillo says that when the land is too hot, a wise man looks for the cool of the waters."

Mann was going for the beach.

Red had taken the first watch that night, his nerves run ragged from Mario's death and their panicky flight from the sun-roasted foothills to the chill of the cliffs and the beach. They had found a place where a small stream ran down across the glittering sand, giving their tired horses something to drink. There was also a cluster of large boulders, like a natural fortress, set well away from the hanging stones among the fringing trees, where the seas crashed in rolling surf. As the tide came in the frothing edges of the waves crept within twenty feet or so of the circle of rocks.

The Indian wormed forward on his belly, smiling as he saw what a good position the whites had picked. It would be interesting to wait and see how long they would stay mewed up inside it. They had water, but precious little food, he thought. And no shelter from the heat.

If he could stop the water . . .

It was too easy. He followed it into the grassy valley and found a place where a few skillfully placed stones and some daubed clay would form a dam, sending the water along a different course, making the fortress a less desirable place to defend.

"Water's gone, Sheriff," hissed Red, some time before midnight. The hours dragged by on halting feet, and the bright moon hung motionless in the star-specked sky.

The old man had been dreaming, muttering and thrashing about in his half-sleep, as he had every night since Red had first met him. Babbling of guns being lost, artillery spiked, and platoons of soldiers butchered in sunken roads. And of Rachel. Always Rachel, his dead wife.

It got on Red's nerves, the old man's pale lips moving all through the night, whispering to himself, the words mostly inaudible, but sometimes clear and shouted, with the crack of command. Red's dislike of Thaddeus Mann was speedily changing to hatred.

"The water, Sheriff," he said again. Again there was no response.

"Water, you stupid old hog-fucker!" he called, the words carrying to Cuchillo Oro, dozing comfortably among the trees a hundred paces away.

"What?"

"The bastard Indian's cut off the water from us," gritted Red angrily.

Mann sat up, blinking around him as if he didn't even know where he was. "What's that, Sergeant?"

"Jesus Christ Almighty, Mann. Get your goddamned brain workin'."

Suddenly the gaping barrel of the heavy pistol was pointing at Red and he gave an involuntary moan of fear, thinking the aged lawman was going to blow him away.

"Insubordinate dog," snarled Mann.

"No, I—"

"No, *sir*, if you please, Sergeant," insisted the old man.

"It's the water, sir, and please put that pistol away."

"Very well, Sergeant. A mite better that report. Might save you from reduction to the ranks and a few nights wagon-wheeling and bayonet-gagging."

"Sure, sir," agreed Red, now totally convinced of the necessity of killing the madman as soon as he could see a clear chance. The only thing that checked him was the knowledge that the ghostly Apache was somewhere out yonder, in the clear-shadowed night. Perhaps it would be better to wait until they'd killed the Indian. Then he could shoot Mann and be away free.

"Now, what's this about the water? Those bluebellies sneaked up on our lines and cut the supply? I'll have those sentries put up against a wall and shot for sleeping in the face of the enemy."

"Enemy? You mean . . . mean the Apache, sir?"

Mann stared at him from bulging eyes. "Indians? You touched by this damned Virginia sun, Sergeant?"

On a good day, downhill with the wind at his heels, Red could just about muster the intelligence of the average water butt. Yet even he realised that there wasn't a lot of point in arguing with Thaddeus Mann now that his brain had completely tipped over into the bloodied past.

"Guess I must have, sir. Must have been them Yankee curs, sneakin' up on us."

"So, there's no water. Plenty in that lake out there," pointing toward the ceaseless waves of the Pacific Ocean, only a few yards from where they sat among the stones.

Red thought fast. "I tried that, sir. It's no good. Fouled."

"Bad water, huh? They play damned dirty, they surely do. No honor. I tell Rachel that. We fight the last great war for the forces of right and decency, Sergeant. We have that on our side, whatever else might befall us."

"Surely do, sir."

"Very well. First rule of being under siege, Sergeant. Keep calm. Calm and under control." His voice rose to an eldritch shriek. "Bring up those damned twelve-pounders, may you rot in hell!" He stopped, as though he were listening to a voice that only he could hear. "All dead? Every mule? Shrapnel? Oh, I detest this war that tears at the heart of this country of ours. Kills it slowly, as it did our town. Our town. Murdered by that Indian."

Red snatched at the word as a drowning man will

reach out for a sliver of wood. "Indian?"

"Cuchillo Oro, Red. He's done this. Damned up the stream, I guess. Wants to watch us sweat it out."

The return to sanity was as sudden as the madness had been. Red pointed toward the black shapes of the packed trees. "Up there?"

"Probably. No chance of goin' after him. Do for us like he did for the kid. Do better followin' a bear into her den. We wait."

"That all?"

"Yeah. Just wait."

The night slipped by slowly. Cuchillo managed to sleep a little, lulled by the ceaseless mumbling rise and fall of the sea. He woke as the false dawn paled the sky, crawling from his hiding place to make sure his prey was still in the stony fortress. Thaddeus Mann was marching up and down across the narrow space within the boulders, carrying a stick of driftwood on his shoulder, pacing out and swinging smartly around, stamping his feet.

It crossed Cuchillo's mind that he might as well leave Mann alive to end his days in descending madness. It was not the way of Indians to harm the insane. Many tribes considered them touched by the spirits, possessed by demons that gave them holy utterances and guarded them from harm. But Cuchillo knew better than that. Knew that the white man could return again to sanity and be once again his sworn enemy.

It had to be done.

* * *

It was a scorchingly hot day, with no shade in the circle of stones. Just the dazzling sun, seeming hotter as it forced its way down through the still air, bouncing off the mirrored sea. A hundred yards out Red saw the fin of a big fish—a shark, he thought—breaking the surface of the ocean, turning with lazy power, and then disappearing again.

"Yanks are quiet."

"What?"

"Quiet out there, Sergeant."

"Oh, yeah. Yeah, sir. They sure are."

Red had decided that he was going to kill Thaddeus Mann during the night. Kill him and then call out to the waiting Indian. He figured that the Apache would maybe let him go if Mann was dead.

Maybe.

Cuchillo watched them through that day, occasionally walking through the quiet green of the trees to kneel and drink, cupping his hands, eyes wary. Insects meandered sleepily about his head, dopey in the serene heat. The Apache was content, knowing that he held his enemy now, with no way of escape. He had decided that he would close in during the hours of darkness, and kill Mann with the golden knife.

Then the spirit of Magnolia Speke would be able to rest easily.

* * *

"Wouldn't be surprised if'n that Indian doesn't come after us tonight, Red."

The ginger-headed man was dozing. He found the old sheriff's returns to lucidity more worrying than his craziness. The latter he could cope with by simply agreeing with everything and calling Mann sir. But when he was sane there was an eagle brightness to the lawman's eyes and a clarity to his mind that frightened the shootist, making him doubt the wisdom of his own plan to murder him that night.

"Cuchillo Oro?"

"Sure. He's the only Indian hereabouts, Red. Better get yourself some shut-eye. Figure we'll make a run for him this night. Get in first."

"The moon?"

"What about it, Sergeant?"

"Jesus!" spat Red, disgustedly. "I mean, I mean that I'm sorry, sir. Just that there was a bright moon during the night."

"Berdan's sharpshooters never needed much of a moon, Sergeant."

"No, sir."

"Nor will we. We will wait until the moon is near gone. Those clouds to the west might well come in from the sea and give us cover later."

"Then what, sir?"

"Go in the woods, Red. Not to take him. Find a good spot. Leave the horses here. Take the rifles. In the end the bastard'll have to break his cover and come to see where we've gone. Try and backtrack us. Then we kill him."

"Sure."

Red decided then that before the moon sank he would kill Thaddeus Mann.

"Sure."

CHAPTER THIRTEEN

Nothing much else happened during the afternoon, except that it grew even hotter. The tantalizing slap of the waves as the tide rose nearer to the circle of boulders nearly drove Red mad, though it seemed to have little or no effect on Thaddeus Mann. The shootist watched the endless small ripples crawl across the sand. They carried tiny black specks of tar, bubbling up from somewhere out in the ocean, the oil carried up on the beach as it had been for thousands of years.

"Guess a taste of that water wouldn't harm a man, huh?"

Mann blinked awake, leathery face dry and puckered like an old sun-spoiled saddle. "Drink the sea?"

"Taste wouldn't signify."

"Maybe, Red."

"Cover me, Sheriff."

"Captain, Sergeant. Your mind's kind of slippin' away, makin' you call me sheriff like that."

"Sure, sir. Sorry."

Mann nodded in a friendly manner. "Know how

the heat affects a young non-com, son. But it's Captain. Captain Thaddeus Mann, Confederate States Army. Leader of some of the best damned infantry in the whole nigger-hatin' world."

"The water, sir?"

"Sure. One taste, Sergeant. Doesn't harm you one jot."

"Then I can—"

Mann went on, ignoring the interruption. "Not a jot, 'ceptin' that you shortly feel a mite thirstier than you did before. So you have another sip. Eases the thirst. Powerful good."

"Maybe if'n I—"

"Then you feel thirstier again. Worse than before. So you take a big swallow. Feels good, Sergeant. Damned good. Down that milk-white swan's throat. Rachel. Asked your kin. Miss Ashley. Cool water. Scorched skin in Richmond. Like a blackened log. No more whiteness. Gone, Red, all gone."

The voice rose from a conversational tone to a wild, raging scream, the sound bringing Cuchillo to the edge of the trees to see what was happening.

"Take it easy," said Red, standing up, hand falling to the butt of his pistol.

"Easy. Easy? Easy! You babble of drinking the salt waters of the great sea! Where monsters dwell in the mysterious deeps! You would surely die. And then?"

He stopped and sat down, abruptly, as if a rug had been pulled from under his feet. His hand reached round to his left hip, the fingers groping, opening and closing as if they sought the gold-tasselled hilt of a sabre. His face had gone blank and he suddenly looked like an old, old man, eyes dim, blinking.

"You all right, Sheriff?" hazarded Red, considering putting a bullet through his skull there and then.

"Yes. See to the horses. They're spooked by something, Red."

The shootist cautiously stood up, his flaming red hair a beacon in the light of the setting sun, reaching toward the two tethered animals. He spoke softly to them, trying to calm them after the lawman's outburst, patting the sheriff's animal and rubbing his hand along the neck of his own. He tried to blow down their nostrils, but they were too spooked.

"Untie the bridles from the rocks," said Thaddeus Mann.

"How's that?"

"Give yourself more room. That's it."

The big Walker banged against his hip as he fought the horses, stooping to loosen the knots and at the same time avoiding their flailing hooves. Even when he'd got them free he was still struggling, hanging on while the old lawman smiled indulgently at him.

"Ride 'em, Red."

"Help me, you damned grey-headed bastard, or we'll lose 'em."

Cuchillo, among the shadows, saw his chance and

took it. He drew the Colt Navy and levered the hammer back, spraying all six rounds toward the huddle of boulders by the sea.

Knowing that he had no hope at that range of doing any real damage.

"Cuchillo says that the sound of death can be as frightening as death itself."

And so it was.

Four out of the six rounds actually struck among the sharp, damp stones, kicking off shards of lethal whining splinters. They kicked around the men and the horses. Bits of jagged rock hit Mann's mount on the neck, drawing a thread of blood. But the pain and shock together were far more devastating in their effect. Both animals screamed and reared, flailing out with their hooves at the man holding them still. Red was caught on the shoulder and knocked spinning backwards over the barrier of stones, rolling in the wet sand.

The lawman tried to grab the bridles but Cuchillo's frightening attack from the blackness of the trees had done exactly what the Apache wanted. As he watched, beginning to reload the warm pistol, he saw the horses vault easily over the stones, both galloping off along the broad expanse of beach. Their hooves drummed on the sand, kicking up small fountains of spray behind them. Mann shouted impotently after the animals, but he was too late.

"They will not come back before the lighting of the sun. Perhaps not then," the Indian said quietly to himself, well satisfied at his success.

* * *

The sun had nearly set. The insects were disappearing as the evening air grew cooler; the sound of the water was clear among the bushes. The shadows from the fortress were lengthening every minute, scraping their way up the beach toward the line of driftwood and weed that marked the highest of watermarks.

It was difficult for Cuchillo to see what was happening. The red ball of the sun was so far down on the horizon that the Pacific cut it almost in half, and its dying fire was still bright enough to dazzle him if he were to look directly into it. By shading his eyes with his crippled right hand he could just make out the dark figures of the two men. High above, the cloud that had appeared earlier in the afternoon was now shredded and torn, vanishing into the foothills of the mountains.

Thaddeus Mann was feeling cold. The effect of the long day without water was to tire him, making him feel his age. And he was finding it hard to keep his mind on the present danger and the present enemy.

The long time without water combined with the dreadful tension was getting to Red. He was lying down on the opposite side of the rock circle from Mann, his lips cracked and sore, weeping blisters all about his face. He was nursing his heavy pistol, rubbing at it with his dirty neckerchief, muttering to himself about what he'd do to the Indian when they caught him.

"Cut it off in fuckin' slices and roast it. Feed it to him. Take his . . ."

"Shut up, Red," said Thaddeus Mann suddenly. "I have had a good gutful of your pitiful whining."

"What?"

"You heard me, I think. Deafness is not among your handicaps."

"Just hold on there."

Cuchillo heard the shout and looked out across the beach, squinting into the glowing redness of the brilliant sunset, barely able to see the men. He began to move a little sideways, picking his way among the trees, trying to find a better angle to see from.

"I will not have this insubordination, Sergeant."

"I ain't your fuckin' sergeant, you damned crazy old man!"

Mann staggered to his feet, exhaustion taking a toll of his speed, reaching for his pistol. In his day he'd been very good, better than anyone that a second-rater like Red had ever seen, and even slowed down he was still better than the shootist expected.

Red had his own handgun already drawn. All he had to do was cock it and fire, Mann being only ten feet away from him.

But he fumbled it.

His thumb, slick with perspiration, slipped on the hammer, making it ease down on half-cock. He was so far ahead of the older man that he still had time to try again, but his eyes were locked to the pistol sliding from Thaddeus Mann's greased holster, his ears filling with the soft click of the gun being readied to fire.

To fire at him.

"Holy Lucifer!" he cried, the gun falling among the stones as he tried to wriggle sideways, away from the raking barrel of the other pistol.

"You dog," said Mann quietly, squeezing on the trigger twice. Three times.

The noise of the explosions brought Cuchillo to the edge of the beach, drawing his own Colt Navy, blinking out. The great cloud of black powder smoke had billowed all around Thaddeus Mann, tinted scarlet by the sun, making it absolutely impossible to see what had happened. But Mann was facing away from him.

Red felt the first bullet hit him in the side, high under his left arm, kicking him over. He slithered among the boulders, his feet in the air. The second shot clipped through the back of his right thigh, punching out a sizable chunk of flesh, making him scream again.

"No! No!"

"Yes, Sergeant," replied Mann.

"No," sobbed Red.

The third shot missed him completely. Mann, blinded by the smoke, failed to see Red scramble up and over the side of the circle of stones, staggering away, running anywhere to get away from the pain and the bullets.

"Yellow, desertin' coward," called Thaddeus Mann, finally catching a glimpse of the lurching man, now close to the edge of the sea.

The old lawman braced himself, holding his right wrist in his left hand, steadying himself for another shot. He pulled on the trigger of the pistol and felt the recoil jar clean to his shoulder.

"God damn it," he muttered, seeing through the tinted cloud of smoke that he'd missed, his aim thrown out by Red's stumbling as he reached the water, running through the shallow waves, kicking up spray all around him.

Cuchillo watched, seeing Mann fire twice more. He grunted and turned away as he saw the last of the six bullets hit the flame-headed man through the top of the skull, stopping him, pitching him face down in the gentle ocean.

Thaddeus Mann nodded his satisfaction. "Save the trouble of a drumhead court-martial," he said, in a clear conversational tone, automatically reloading his pistol. He reached for his ammunition pouch at his belt, slightly surprised to find that he wasn't wearing his army uniform.

But his mind was growing more clouded. He closed his eyes and saw a picket fence splintered by a thousand bullets, with a young boy's corpse draped over it, one hand almost severed from the arm, and a stream flowing with blood.

"First Bull Run," he whispered.

He sat down, Cuchillo Oro quite forgotten, the dead man that floated in the sea gone from his mind.

CHAPTER FOURTEEN

During that long evening both Cuchillo Oro and Thaddeus Mann waited for the other to make a move. But as the light faded, crimson in the west, the bright moon came easing out, throwing sharp shadows from the spread body of Red lying on its side where the tide had left it.

During that long evening both Cuchillo Oro and Thaddeus Mann slipped into restless sleep. Though they would never know it, both dreamed about their dead wives.

For the Apache it was a familiar nightmare, a grim harking back to the night when he had seen his wife and young baby butchered by the cavalry officer, Cyrus Pinner. The handsome, arrogant, laughing face. In his dream he stood alone on top of a mountain of gleaming crystal, with polished sides so smooth that it was impossible to climb down them.

And Pinner was there.

In his sleep Cuchillo gripped the rough hilt of the golden knife and his face tightened in remembered anger and bitterness at the wrecking of his life and his happiness.

There was a strange bird flying across the side of the mountain, its silver beak glittering, its wings flapping with a soundless, heavy beat. Cuchillo watched the bird, and then, without his being aware of having moved, he was at the bottom of the mountain, and Pinner was standing on a ledge some twenty feet above him, holding Cuchillo's son, Troubled Night. And the Apache's wife was at the shoulder of the white man.

They both laughed at him, mocking him for being unable to climb the glassy slope to reach them. Chipeta pointed her finger at Cuchillo and then reached inside the white man's breeches, pulling out his penis, stroking it, and calling to her husband that he was so well endowed. In his fitful dream Cuchillo lowered his own pants to show that her taunts were not true, but his penis was gone, the skin smooth and unbroken where it should have been.

Pinner laughed at him, taking Chipeta's shining black hair and tugging her down to her knees in front of him, making her take him in her mouth and pleasure him.

He jerked his hips at her face, mouth torn in a rictus of lust. Cuchillo tried to climb the rocks, but they were more slippery than ice and he fell back. He drew his knife from the sheath and throwing it up at Pinner with all his anger and hatred.

But it turned in his hand, becoming a small white

dove that flew up and away, settling on the shoulder of the soldier. Pinner ejaculated in Chipeta's mouth and she leaned over the ledge and spat it down into Cuchillo's upturned face, but it was dry, gray ash that filled his eyes and made him cry out in horror and shock, waking him.

For Thaddeus Mann, the night also brought hideous phantoms, gibbering from the graves in his past.

He was on a beach, but not like that one in California. This was scattered with chunks of pack ice, broken and jagged, reflecting rainbow lights. The sea was a dull grey color, heaving gently, its surface frozen. And he was walking along it, finding it hard to lift his feet in the rutted slush.

Behind him he could hear the sound of an animal. A horse, cantering very slowly. He looked round and there were dozens of animals, all purest white, each one ridden by a soldier. Each man's hand gripped a standard bearing a gold field with the letters C.S.A. on it in flaming crimson.

"Rachel," he said, his lips moving in his sleep. "Oh, my Rachel."

She led the squadron, her long hair blowing in a wind. But there was no wind.

"Rachel!" he called, yet no sound came from his throat. White breath plumed from his open mouth as he tried to call her again, but there was still nothing. The horses were coming closer to him, heading straight at him.

Mann turned and tried to run, but the ice and

snow snatched at his feet and he fell, rolling on his back and staring up, seeing a sky that was crisscrossed with clouds, and a sun that was moving, traveling across the heavens as he watched it.

"Spare me, Rachel!" But there was no noise, no words that reached his ears.

"All the horses are dead here, sir," called one of the men riding behind Rachel, and this time Thaddeus heard the words clearly.

He managed to rise to his knees and then his wife was on top of him, riding him down as if he hadn't existed, the legs of the stallion kicking him back again, knocking him unconscious.

When the blackness passed he was still on the beach, kneeling, his arms gripped with a ferocious strength by two of the blank-faced soldiers, forcing him to stillness. His shirt was torn apart, baring his chest to the keen wind that had risen from the leaden sea.

And Rachel was there, smiling at him, her eyes blue as the sky in a Montana summer. She wore a long flowing gown of pale lilac silk, cut so low at the bodice that he could see the soft swell of her gentle breasts.

"Thaddeus," she whispered.

"Help me. Make them free me, dearest," he said, but the words became choked and strangled so that all that came from his lips was a succession of muffled grunts.

"You took your guns and drums, Thaddeus."

"Yes."

"And went for a soldier."

"My duty," he tried to say.

"Left me to die, alone, dearest Thaddeus. So alone alone alone."

The pressure on his arms and shoulders was becoming intolerable but the troopers holding him might have been cast from bronze for all their relaxation.

"Alone, darling. While you were a hero. Such a brave and happy man."

"I have been alone, Rachel, these long years. Alone and dying from the moment of your passing."

But she heard nothing. She bent over him, stroking his face with tender fingers. He saw that she wore a short knife at her belt. A tiny, thin-bladed skinning knife, with a hilt of gold.

"Poor Thaddeus. I have found you guilty and sentence you to live forever."

"No."

She put her mouth to his, and kissed him.

Among the boulders by the warm Pacific, Thaddeus Mann rolled in his sleep, one hand clutching at the soft sand, scooping it and crushing it between his fingers. His eyelids flickered with the intensity of his nightmare and he moaned quietly.

Rachel's tongue pressed between his cold lips and he tried to struggle away from her, but her long nails dug into his cheeks, holding him still. Her lips were hot, the tip of her tongue probing inside his mouth like a needle of fire, searing him.

"Fare thee well, husband," she said, pulling away

from him, and he saw that she held the knife in her right hand.

"Please . . ."

"As my will, Thaddeus, so must it be."

While his arms were held spread, she passed the knife backwards and forwards across his naked chest, finally thrusting its point in, so that he felt the chill metal slide between his fifth and sixth ribs on the left side of his body. His dead wife twisted the hilt with savage force, so that it tore his heart apart. Blood filled his mouth and he fell, released by the silent soldiers, face down in the ice and salt snow.

With his death, Thaddeus Mann woke up, and saw that it was nearly dawn.

There was a grey mist far out on the sea's face, and a grey dawn breaking. Far off, near a jagged promontory of rock, Cuchillo could see the two horses, quietly grazing side by side, where the grass came down beyond the edge of the trees.

Red's body still lay where the receding tide had left it, his bright hair now oddly dulled. Thaddeus Mann was kneeling on the near side of the natural fort, the barrel of his rifle protruding in the direction of the hiding Apache.

From the way the watery sun was trying to break through the high clouds over the foothills behind Cuchillo, he guessed that it was going to be a fine day.

The Apache felt tired and unwell. The days of ease and comfort in the city of the white men had taken a toll far deeper than he had imagined. Then the shock of the killing in the theatre and the chase to the sea. He had eaten little and drunk sparingly but his stomach felt heavy and full. The dreams of the last fitful night had also depressed him, and he looked out across the strip of beach at his enemy.

He even considered walking away to his horse, mounting up and riding off, letting everything lie where it had fallen.

When he had been a young warrior, the diminutive John Hedges had told him that revenge belonged to the white man's Jesus Christ, the Lord. It had seemed unlikely then, and the years had taught Cuchillo that the idea was nonsense. He doubted that John Hedges believed it any more.

"It must finish here," he said to himself, checking the pistol at his hip, trying to work out a plan that would enable him to reach the old man without running into instant death from his long gun.

Time was on his side, though there was no way of knowing when someone else might pass by this desolate beach. If they were white they would certainly side with Mann, and he might have to withdraw. And it would all begin over again.

Along the beach the horses were moving on closer, staying together.

"Cuchillo Oro!"

Peering between the trunks of the cool damp trees, the Indian watched and waited.

"I want this ended, son. I had troubles with my

head . . . I ain't been thinkin' real straight. Now there's you and me, boy. Let's to it."

"I have no long gun," shouted Cuchillo.

"I got me two. Mine and that scum of a sergeant's that—I mean, Red's. Two rifles."

Cuchillo still waited, letting the silence stretch out between them for the space of fifty heart-beats.

"If'n you want to end it right, I'll throw them out back, clean to the sea."

The tide was again creeping in over the shimmering sand, within fifty feet of the furthest of the sheltering boulders.

"Throw them."

"You'll come for a shoot-out?"

"Cuchillo gives his word."

"Indian's word?" There was a touch of the old wryness and hardness in the lawman's tone.

"It was the whites that taught Indians how to tell their crook-tongued lies," retorted the big Apache.

"Here they go! Red's first." A rifle, like a frail black stick, whirling in the air and splashing down in the Pacific. "And mine." Again the fountain of white spray.

It crossed the mind of Cuchillo that the wily old man might also have the kid's rifle, tucked away ready for use.

"Now stand and come out, so I can see there is no trick."

"Trustin' son of a bitch, aren't you?"

"I am still alive."

142

"Not for long, son. This is truly the end of the tracks for you."

The horses were only a hundred yards away, nuzzling at each other, ignoring the men's voices.

Thaddeus Mann stood slowly up, stepping stiffly over the stones, standing in full view of Cuchillo, looking blindly into the scrub. Staring a full fifty feet away from where the Indian was waiting.

"I'm here, boy."

Cuchillo studied him, seeing the stretched hands, the lifted arms, watching as Mann took a couple of hesitant steps towards the trees. It was difficult to see how he could be hiding a rifle.

"I come," he replied.

Thaddeus turned, surprised to see him appear further along the beach than he'd thought. He reached down out of habit to check that the retaining thong was clear of the hammer of his pistol.

"You ready for this, boy?"

"I have been ready for many months."

"No words. Draw when you're content."

Cuchillo nodded, wiping the palms of his hands against the sides of his cotton trousers. He reached up and tucked a few strands of his long black hair into the scarf that served him as a headband. Magnolia's scarf, still carrying the faint whisper of her scent.

Not far out to sea another of the great whales surfaced with a hissing of breath, turning and flinging its huge grey tail, snapping it down on the water with a crack like a whip. Mann looked round for a moment, then back to face Cuchillo, a half-smile on his lips at the interruption.

"It sounded like Blessed Christ!"

The noise had spooked the two horses and they had broken into a gallop, heading down the beach, directly toward Mann. He waved his arms at them, changing their angle so that they were headed into the gap between the lawman and the trees.

Seeing that they might give him the chance that he needed to beat the better shootist, Cuchillo started to move in fast, running toward Mann, drawing his pistol as he ran. The old sheriff stood as if someone had put nails through his feet, gaping at the horses galloping at him.

"You said they was all dead!" he screamed, pulling out his own handgun, fanning at the hammer, the bullets howling through the morning stillness, none of them coming within ten feet of the advancing Indian.

The animals were only forty yards off, their hooves drumming, kicking up a cloud of sand behind them, heads thrown back, one neighing its fear at the burst of gunfire in front of them.

In the excitement Cuchillo had lost track of the number of shots that Mann had fired. It was four or five. Just before the horses came between them there was another shot, the bullet so close it seemed to tug at the sleeve of his thin shirt.

As the animals charged past, eyes rolled back with fear, the earth shook and Cuchillo lost sight of

Thaddeus Mann. Which meant that the white man must also have lost sight of him.

So, instead of running forward, or trying to dodge, the Apache hurled himself down into the disturbed sand, pistol cocked and ready, looking for Mann.

"Save me, Rachel!" came an eerie, wavering voice, ragged in the sudden stillness. A voice empty with a lonely terror and laid over with clear madness.

Thaddeus Mann was kneeling, the gun still in his right hand, peering about him for the wraiths that had etched blank fear across his face. For a moment Cuchillo wondered whether he had fired five or six, but it didn't much matter. The white man was less than twenty yards away and the Indian's own Navy Colt still held six loads.

"Bring up the twelve-pounders, here!" yelled the old man, looking straight at Cuchillo, but not seeming to see him.

The Apache aimed the gun and pulled the trigger, seeing the bullet strike home in the center of Thaddeus Mann's chest, close by the faded patch on his jacket where the silver star had once been pinned. Blood came, and the white man lurched back, dropping the pistol in the sand, keeping himself from falling with a tremendous effort of will.

Eyes clearing, seeing the Indian, even managing a half smile.

"You bastard," he muttered, but without malice. "You done for me."

As Cuchillo watched him, Mann reached for his own dropped pistol, picking it up.

Five rounds or six.

It didn't signify. Cuchillo had five more. He levered back on the Colt, and the gun jammed. The cylinder wouldn't turn all the way to bring the hammer in line with the cap.

Five rounds or six?

Life or death.

Thaddeus Mann pointed his own pistol, watched by Cuchillo, knowing that nothing on earth could save him if there was one more bullet in the gun of the white man. The pistol seemed too heavy for the dying Thaddeus, and he labored to hold it steady.

"So long, son. You done good," he said, and pulled the trigger.

The dry click of an empty pistol.

Six rounds fired.

"Bang," whispered the old man, the gun falling silently to the soft sand. He fell on his face, blood dark and gleaming across his back.

Cuchillo stood up and looked down at the body of his enemy.

Glad that the War, at last, was finished.

The sun was burning away the clouds across the Pacific Ocean. It was going to be a good day.

SPECIAL PREVIEW

The blazing Western series by the author of the bestselling EDGE series

George G. Gilman
ADAM STEELE

The adventures of Adam Steele are written by the author of our bestselling Edge *series, who has created another brand of blazing Westerns to show the way it really was in the West . . . a grim and gritty view unpolished by history, untamed by time!*

Outraged over his father's murder, Adam Steele rides to his destiny on a bloody trail of revenge and retribution. He carries with him a rifle bearing the dedication that is his inspiration: "To Benjamin P. Steele, with gratitude, Abraham Lincoln." And Steele won't stop until he finds his father's killers . . . and any other killer who crosses his path!

The following is an edited version of the first few chapters, as we are introduced to Adam Steele*:

Adam Steele reined his bay gelding to a halt at the crest of a rise and split his mouth in a gentle smile as he sur-

*Copyright by George G. Gilman.

veyed the lights of the city spread before him. It had been a long ride from Richmond and he spent a few relaxed moments in quiet contemplation of the end of the journey. Then he sighed and heeled the horse forward down the gentle incline that led into Washington.

He rode upright, but not tall in the Western saddle. He was just a shade over five feet six inches in height, his build compact rather than slight, and suggested adequate strength instead of power. Like so many young men who have survived the bitter fighting of the war just ended, he looked older than his actual years, which totaled twenty-eight. He had a long face with regular features that gave him a nondescript handsomeness. His mouthline was gentle, his nose straight, and his coal black eyes honest. His hair was prematurely gray with only a few hanks of dark red to show its former coloration. It was trimmed neat and short, and this was the only obvious sign of the five years he had spent in the army of the Confederate States.

The city was very quiet as Steele entered the streets of its southern section and he was mildly surprised at this. Washington was the capital of the victorious northern states and he had expected it still to be in the throes of triumphant revelry even this long after Lee's surrender. But he did not give too much thought to the matter, for he had another, more important subject on his mind. He had no trouble finding his way to his destination, for he had been a frequent visitor to the city in pre-war days and little had changed during the intervening years.

It was not until he turned onto Tenth Street that he pulled up short in surprise. The street was as quiet as all the others had been, but there was a difference. Where the others had been deserted, this one was crowded with people. The great majority of them were huddled together in a large group before a house diagonally across the street from the darkened façade of Ford's Theatre. Occasionally, one or more of the silent spectators would drift away from the crowd. One such was an old woman who stepped unwittingly in front of Steele's horse as he urged the animal forward. She looked at the rider, showing no emotion at almost being trampled. Deep shock dwelled behind her moist eyes.

"What's happening here, ma'am?" Steele asked, his voice smoothed by a Virginia drawl as he touched his hat brim with a gloved hand.

The old woman blinked, and a tear was squeezed from the corner of each eye. "Mr. Lincoln," she replied tremulously. "They've shot Mr. Lincoln."

Under different circumstances, Steele knew he might have felt a surge of joy and expectation that the event could signal new hope for the South to rise against defeat. But he had come to Washington determined to forget the past and adjust himself to the best future he could make. Even so, he had difficulty in injecting a degree of the mournful into his voice as he asked, "Is the President dead?"

The old woman shook her head. "He's dying. Won't last out the night, they say."

Steele took a final look down the street, then jerked over the reins to angle his horse toward Elmer's Barroom. It was not in complete darkness, for a dim light flickered far back in one of the windows. After he had looped the reins over the hitching rail at the edge of the sidewalk, he approached the doors and they swung open in front of him.

"We're closed, mister," Elmer announced as the newcomer crossed the threshold. "Mark of respect for the President."

The doors squeaked closed behind Steele and he halted abruptly. He saw Elmer standing behind the bar, using the turned-down light of a single kerosene lamp to count the night's takings. "I just heard," he said, moving toward the bar. "After getting news like that, a man needs a drink. Whiskey."

He pulled up short again as something brushed against his shoulder. As he looked up, he could see the limply hanging form of a dead man. The body revolved slowly from where he had collided with a dangling leg. "Turn up the lamp, bartender," he said softly.

Elmer continued to chink loose change, taking it from his apron pocket and stacking it on the bartop. "Told you, mister, the place is closed up for the night," he growled.

"You don't turn up that lamp, I'll kill you," Steele said, his drawling voice still pitched low. But it was high on menace.

Elmer's head snapped up and he peered intently through the darkness toward the newcomer. He could not see Steele clearly and it was for this reason he reached out and turned up the wick. His free hand dragged a Manhattan Navy Model out from beneath the bar. When the pool of light had spread far enough to illuminate Steele and the hanging man, the revolver was cocked and aimed. "You don't look capable, mister," Elmer said, noting that Steele wore no gunbelt and his hands were empty.

Steele was staring up at the swollen face of the old man. His own features were empty of expression and when he turned to look at Elmer and started to walk toward him he still gave no outward sign of what he was thinking. "What happened here?" he asked, the threat missing from his low tones. But neither was he concerned with the pointing gun in the bartender's hands. He glanced casually to his right and saw a bearded old timer with a bloody forehead climbing painfully to his feet. Then to the left, where a sleeping drunk was just a lumpy shadow against a deeper shadow beneath the table.

Elmer's sullen eyes met Steele's open stare, then took in at close range the man's easy-going features and unprovoking build. He lumped all this together with the lack of visible weapons and decided his unwanted customer had a tough mouth but nothing with which to back it up. He put the gun down beneath the bar and started to dig for more coins. "A guy blasted the President over at the theatre," he rasped. "Got clean away." He nodded toward the man hanging from the beam. "That guy passed the gun to the murderer. Didn't have the sense to take it on the lam." A sour grin twisted his mouth. "Me and a few others kinda forced him to hang around."

The old timer was leaning his elbows on the bar, nursing his broken head in the palms of his hands. "Weren't no proof of that!" he snapped, without looking up. "Ed Binns and his pals just up and hanged the old man on account of what you told 'em."

Elmer glowered hatefully at the old timer. "He give the gun to Booth, I'm telling you," he snarled.

"And you can give me a drink," Steele said.

Elmer sighed, seemed about to refuse, then swung around and swept a shot glass and bottle from the shelf behind him. He set the glass on the bartop and poured the right measure without looking.

Steele proffered no money, and neither did he reach for the drink. "What if you were wrong?" he asked.

Elmer banged the bottle down angrily. "Just drink your drink and get out so I can close up," he ordered. "I weren't wrong."

"You were wrong," Steele said. With his left hand, Steele tugged at his ear lobe. His right hand came fast out of the pocket on that side of the jacket and Elmer's eyes widened with terror as he saw the tiny two-shot derringer clutched in the fist. The gun went off with a small crack. The shattered whiskey bottle made a louder noise. Elmer fell backward, crashing against the display shelf. His hands clutched at his bulbous stomach. Small shards of broken glass glittered against the dark stains of whiskey covering his apron. He looked down at himself and gasped when he saw the blood oozing between his fingers.

"His name was Benjamin Steele. And my name is Adam Steele," the man said softly. "That was my father you killed."

The pain had had time to reach Elmer now, and it overflowed his eyes in the form of tears as he brought his head up to look at the man he had so badly misjudged. Steele held the shocked stare of the other, as he slid the derringer back into his pocket and used his left hand to draw out a match. He struck it on his thumbnail and in the sudden flare of yellow light his eyes seemed not to be as one with the rest of his features. For the lines of his face had a composed, innocuous set—while the eyes, pulled wide, blazed with a seemingly unquenchable fury.

Then the flaring match was arced forward. Elmer emitted a strangled sob of horror, throwing up his hands. The match sailed between them and bounced against his chest. It fell to the floor, but not before a fragile flame licked up from the whiskey-sodden material of his shirt. He beat at it with a blood-stained hand, the motion fanning the fire. Within a terrifying few seconds, as the fury died within Steele, the bartender's massive body was enveloped in searing flames. As shreds of charred clothing fell from him and the intense heat swept over his naked skin, his sobs became strangled cries. He threw himself to the floor and began to roll backward and forward as he beat at the hungry flames. But the whiskey-soaked sawdust only added fuel to the agonizing fire.

The old timer's horror at the lynching was nothing compared to the revulsion he felt as he watched Elmer's pitifully ineffectual attempts to beat out the flames. But he made no effort to intervene, conscious of the evil lurking beneath the deceptively gentle surface of the young man standing beside him.

"Innocent man getting lynched," Steele said, still softly. "Fair burns a man up, doesn't it?"

* * *

The hole was almost as deep as Adam Steele was tall. Reverently he lowered the stiff body of the old man into the bare earth, not looking down into the trench until the corpse was completely covered. Then he worked furiously to shovel the rest of the dirt onto the grave. His fury grew as he realized he wouldn't be able to place a marker on the site.

He gazed once again at the still-smoking ruins of the Steele home. Only a few items were worth salvaging. Souvenirs of better, peaceful days. But Adam would only take one reminder. An unusual weapon, a Colt Hartford sporting rifle, six-shot revolving percussion, .44 caliber, given to his father by the President. The barrel was covered with soot, and the rosewood stock was slightly charred, but the action worked smoothly.

Now Lincoln and Ben Steele were both dead. Two fine lives extinguished by madness . . . two burials marked the beginning of an unending and blood-soaked vengeance trail for Adam Steele.